"You're still ___ happy, are you?"

Cale's observation came after ten minutes of complete silence.

Anstey shrugged. "How can I be?" she asked tonelessly. "It isn't right that your mother doesn't know Rosie is Lester's child. I've had to go along with you and deceive your mother. Quite honestly, Cale, I don't like it."

"Do you think I like it any better?" he asked. "But I've explained why it has to be this way. Look, try not to worry," he said, stretching out a hand to pat one of hers. "You and I are in this together. I won't make a move without consulting you first."

Anstey wasn't quite sure how she felt about being in "anything" with Cale. Hard as granite, yet concerned about his aging parent, Cale Quartermaine was the most confusing man! Had he taken Anstey's feelings into account at all?

Jessica Steele first tried her hand at writing romance novels at her husband's encouragement two years after they were married. She fondly remembers the day her first novel was accepted for publication. "Peter mopped me up, and neither of us cooked that night," she recalls. "We went out to dinner." She and her husband live in a hundred-year-old cottage in Worcestershire, and they've traveled to many fascinating places—such as China, Japan, Mexico and Denmark—that make wonderful settings for her books.

Books by Jessica Steele

Don't miss any of our special offers. Write to us at the following address for information on our newest releases.

Harlequin Reader Service
901 Fuhrmann Blvd., P.O. Box 1397, Buffalo, NY 14240
Canadian address: P.O. Box 603,
Fort Erie, Ont. L2A 5X3

Unfriendly Alliance

Jessica Steele

Harlequin Books

TORONTO • NEW YORK • LONDON
AMSTERDAM • PARIS • SYDNEY • HAMBURG
STOCKHOLM • ATHENS • TOKYO • MILAN

Original hardcover edition published in 1987
by Mills & Boon Limited

ISBN 0-373-02916-0

Harlequin Romance first edition June 1988

CHAPTER ONE

THE BABY started to cry, *again*. Anstey was feeling so down that she could easily have cried too. Rousing herself from her dejection, she went to the bedroom and lifted Rosie from her cot.

'I know I'm doing this all wrong, and that I probably shouldn't pick you up every time you whimper,' she crooned to the tiny two-month-old scrap, 'but why shouldn't someone spoil you? Your mother's disappeared, your father couldn't care less, and fatty, ratty Kenneth downstairs has a decided aversion to hearing you exercise your lungs at full throttle.'

Anstey walked the baby up and down for a while until, to her relief, Rosie stopped crying. Fearing to put her down in case she started off once more, she carried her into the sitting-room and sat down with her.

As she cradled the baby to her, Anstey's worries were soon on the same old treadmill. What was she going to do? It was nearly three weeks now since Joanna had gone—when was she coming back?

Troubled about her dear friend, she glanced down and saw that Rosie had fallen asleep. 'It's all your fault,' she whispered gently. But it was not Rosie Tresilla Quartermaine's fault. She hadn't asked to come into the world. Indeed, had that rat Lester Quartermaine had his way, she would never have been born. He had not been pleased when Joanna had told him she was pregnant. His answer was that she should have the pregnancy aborted. Joanna had refused.

Anstey knew her friend had hoped that, once the baby arrived, Lester would learn to love the child and that, since he professed to be very much in love with Joanna, he would ask her to marry him. It had not worked out that way.

Poor Joanna, she was so much in love with Lester that she had continued to believe it would all come right. Doubts had started to set in, however, when she had telephoned him from the maternity ward to tell him that they had a lovely daughter.

'What else is new?' he'd answered heartlessly, his tone so uncaring that Joanna, in relaying the conversation to Anstey, had broken down and wept.

Anstey was slow to anger, and until then she had quite liked Lester. He was always full of fun, and she too had believed that deep down he truly loved her friend. But when Joanna had finished telling her of his heartlessness, she had been all for charging round to his flat to give forth along the lines that it was about time he faced up to his responsibilities.

'Please don't, it'll only make things worse,' Joanna had cried when Anstey had been too incensed to keep quiet about what she intended to do. 'For my sake, don't meddle.'

So she had swallowed her anger, and had not meddled. She couldn't refrain from meddling on another front, though. With not a word or a visit from Lester, Joanna was discharged from hospital, but her mind was so much on him that it looked as though the baby was going to lose out. Gone was the eagerness with which she had looked forward to the baby's arrival. So much so that at times Anstey had to coax her to show an interest in the fragile bundle.

Anstey took two weeks out of her holiday entitlement to help out. But at the end of those two weeks, she found herself more in charge of attending to the baby's requirements than merely assisting.

Which was perhaps why Joanna must have felt Anstey could cope when she had a resurgence of her old habit of 'lighting out' when things got too much for her.

Anstey had been back at work for three weeks when she returned home one evening to find that Rosie had been left with Hazel, their downstairs neighbour, and that Joanna had gone.

Anstey and Joanna had grown up living next door to each other, so in a flash she was reminded of her friend's teenage penchant for taking off when the trauma of her wretched home life became too much for her to handle. The fact that Joanna knew she would be in deeper hot water from her tyrannical stepfather had not mattered when, unable to take any more verbal abuse, she would just— leave.

But Anstey had thought Joanna's disappearing act was a thing of the past. They had come to London together four years ago and Joanna, her emotions soon on a more even keel hadn't once shown any sign of wanting to 'get away from it all'.

Rosie stirred in her arms but did not wake, and Anstey's thoughts went back to the night before Joanna had gone. Still trying to get her to think more of the baby than of Lester, she had reminded her friend that if she didn't wish to break the law, then she couldn't leave it much later before she registered her baby's birth.

'You haven't changed your mind about the names you chose if she were to be a girl?' she had asked, remembering happier times when, months in advance, they had discussed the merits and demerits of possible names.

'Rosie Tresilla Quartermaine, she'll be,' Joanna had responded.

Encouraged to think that Joanna was taking more of an interest in the baby, Anstey had arrived home the following evening to discover just how wrong she had been.

Hazel Davies from the ground-floor flat had met her in the hall. Hazel was a pleasant woman, married to Kenneth for ten years and desperately yearning for a child—a yearning which her husband did not share.

About to give her a cheerful greeting in passing, Anstey saw something in Hazel's expression which made her amend her greeting to 'What . . .?'

'The baby's asleep on my bed,' Hazel said quickly. And, just as quickly, 'Joanna's gone.'

'Gone!'

Hurriedly Hazel had explained how Joanna had appeared at her door that afternoon, clutching a suitcase in one hand and the baby in her arm. 'She said she had to get away, and asked if I'd mind little Rosie until you came home. Naturally I said I'd have the baby with pleasure, but . . .'

'Did she say where she was going?' Anstey butted in, recalling instantly Joanna's old compulsion to get away when things became too much for her.

'I tried to question her, but I couldn't get another thing out of her save for repeating that she had to go. I've given Rosie her bottle, by the way,' Hazel thought to mention.

'I'd better take her.' Anstey weathered her stunned feelings to follow Hazel into her flat.

'If you would,' said Hazel, starting to look a shade uncomfortable. 'Kenneth will be home in about fifteen minutes.'

Anstey took Rosie up to the flat she shared with Joanna, well aware that Kenneth, whom it was not unknown to hear yell 'Can't you keep that kid quiet?' would not take kindly to having Rosie in possession of his bed when he came home.

Her thoughts going nineteen to the dozen, Anstey laid

the sleeping Rosie down, and took out the telephone directory. It seemed obvious to her that with Joanna so much in love with Lester Quartermaine, if she'd told anyone where she was going, it would be him.

She found his number without difficulty. It was directly under the bold print of Quartermaine Holdings, the firm owned by Lester's hard-as-rock brother. Anstey began to dial, wasting barely a thought on Cale Quartermaine. She had never met him, but any man who could so callously end his own brother's career a couple of years ago by booting Lester out of his firm was not, in her opinion, worth knowing. But both Quartermaine brothers went from her mind when, suddenly centring her thoughts on Joanna again, Anstey realised that she could be doing her friend the greatest disservice by trying to find her! Quickly, she put the phone back on its rest.

Past experience showed that Joanna always came home when she'd recharged her emotional batteries. Besides which, if Joanna ran true to her old form, she'd shun like the plague the idea of letting anyone know where she was, or of going to anyone who might pressure her into returning before she was ready.

An hour later, Anstey was so worried that she was having to forcibly remind herself that to ring Lester would be the worst disservice she could do her friend. Then, suddenly, the phone in the flat rang.

Like a shot she was over to it, picking it up to hear her friend's voice. 'Joanna! Where are you?' she cried in relief.

'I—need—some time, by myself,' Joanna answered flatly.

'Yes, I understand that,' said Anstey quickly; she was as close to her as a sister but she was aware that occasionally they both needed their own space. 'But ...'

'Will you look after Rosie for me, until I get myself sorted out?' Joanna asked, and confessed in her usual open way, 'I wasn't going to ring you, only it came to me suddenly that ...' she broke off, and there was a bitter note in her voice, when she resumed, ' ... that one of the baby's parents should show some sense of responsibility for her.'

'Yes, of course I'll look after her,' Anstey speedily assured her, but bitterness was so unlike Joanna that she just had to ask, 'What's—gone wrong, Jo?'

'What else, you mean?' replied Joanna, and broke down completely as she revealed, 'Nothing—ex-except that L-Lester is denying p-paternity.'

'He's—what!' Anstey gasped, knowing for a fact that Lester had been Joanna's one and only lover. 'Has he said so?'

'It amounts to the same thing,' Joanna said, struggling to regain her self-control. 'I went to register Rosie's birth this morning—as you reminded me I should. But I found out that, although I could give her Lester's surname, or any surname I fancied for that matter, unless Lester agreed, I couldn't have him named on her birth certificate as her father.'

'Lester wouldn't agree?' Anstey asked, fearing the worst.

'I rang him,' said Joanna, and started to cry again. 'I asked him to come and meet me at the registrar's so he could sign whatever he had to sign. But he—he—said th-that since he'd never wanted the baby in the f-first place, he was damn sure he wasn't going to sign for it.'

'Oh—love,' Anstey choked, as shocked as Joanna must have been that Lester was quite prepared to let his child go through life with no officially listed father.

Seconds ticked away as Joanna made fresh attempts to stop crying. 'I need time,' she then reiterated. 'Time to think Lester out of my system. Time to accept—even though I've registered Rosie with his surname—that it's all over between him and me. I need time, Anstey,' she said, 'to get myself together to be able to come home and take on the responsibility of being a single parent.'

Anstey was not sure that she wasn't going to start weeping herself, and freely she invited, 'Take as long as you like, love.'

'The way I feel now,' threatened Joanna with a valiant attempt at humour, 'it'll take a year.'

'What are friends for?' Anstey teased, in her determination that Joanna should feel no pressure from her.

'I should have added your name to Rosie Tresilla,' Joanna replied gratefully.

'Poor mite!' Anstey, christened Anastasia, responded. 'She'll be glad you didn't.'

'Keep her safe for me, Anstey,' Joanna said solemnly, and waited only to receive Anstey's fervent promise, then sighed, 'I'll need her when I get back,' and rang off.

Believing she would be back in a few days, Anstey rang her boss the next morning. Mr Sallis was not very thrilled that at such short notice she wanted the rest of the week off, but he finally agreed that she could take the time out of her dwindling holiday allowance.

Rosie proved as fretful as ever that morning, but eventually she stopped crying to take a nap for long enough for Anstey to pop down to tell Hazel that she had heard from Joanna, and that Joanna would soon be back.

Away for a matter of minutes, Anstey returned upstairs to tidy up what was rapidly becoming a very cramped apartment. Perhaps their landlord had known a thing or two when he had stipulated 'No children' in their tenancy agreement, she mused. For where once the flat with its twin-bedded bedroom had been adequate for two adults, the essential equipment for a baby's wellbeing had shown that the arrival of one tiny infant made it overcrowded.

Anstey was tackling the daily wash when Rosie awoke and started crying. She cried on and on, and when nothing would pacify her, Anstey began to get seriously worried.

Frazzled herself by midday, she found her promise to Joanna to keep Rosie safe mingled with a feeling of helplessness. Her experience of babies had been non-existent until Rosie had come along. What if the baby was not merely fretful—but ill!

Early that afternoon Anstey took Rosie to see Dr Favell, the caring if slightly old-fashioned general practitioner with whom Joanna had registered when she had discovered she was pregnant.

'You're worrying unnecessarily,' he pronounced, after giving the baby a thorough examination and hearing that she was gaining weight. 'She's perfectly normal and perfectly healthy. This young lady doesn't have a problem,' he said with a sympathetic smile, 'you do. You,' he went on, 'or rather, Miss Keeble, has been unlucky enough to produce a crier. How is Miss Keeble, incidentally?' he asked.

'She's gone away for a few days,' she answered but, not wanting him to think her friend an uncaring mother, she felt bound to add, 'She's not—very happy—at the moment.'

'Oh,' he murmured, 'and why's that?'

Anstey felt a trifle uncomfortable, but while she would be loyal to Joanna to the death, she felt no such loyalty for Lester Quartermaine, only anger. 'Her boyfriend—her ex-boyfriend . . .' she began in confidence.

A short while later the doctor, by sympathetic questioning, had received a broad outline of why Joanna was not very happy just then.

'You said Miss Keeble telephoned you last evening,' he detailed. 'How was she—weepy?'

'She has every cause,' Anstey replied.

Dr Favell put Rosie's documents back in their envelope, and stood up. 'Go home and try not to fret about this bundle of noise,' he said, chucking Rosie under the chin. 'Nor Miss Keeble either,' he added, noting Anstey's worried brow. 'Many young mothers, I promise you, would give a right arm to be able to decamp from a crying offspring for a few days.'

Anstey came away from the surgery feeling much better able to cope now that she knew Rosie was just being a crosspatch for the sake of it.

When Sunday arrived, though, and Joanna had not, Anstey started to get anxious about something else. Mr Sallis would blow his top if she had to ring him tomorrow to ask for more time off work. Yet if Joanna was not home, short of taking the baby to work with her, there was no way she was going to be able to put in an appearance at the offices of Elton Diesel.

It was going on for three that afternoon when Anstey heard someone coming up the stairs. In a flash she was over at the door, pulling it wide.

'Sorry, it's only me,' said Hazel, on seeing the crestfallen look which Anstey was not quick enough to hide. 'Joanna not back yet?'

'She obviously needs more time than I thought,' Anstey replied, managing to produce a smile as she invited Hazel in.

'Kenneth's gone to visit his mother,' Hazel volunteered, at the same time extracting a pink fluffy toy from the paper bag she held. 'I bought this yesterday, but haven't had a chance to come up before.'

'Rosie's just fallen asleep,' Anstey told her, and guessed that Hazel did not want Kenneth to know about her small gift, when she remarked,

'Why is it that she always manages to fall asleep when he goes out?'

'I know her crying disturbs him, but I'm sure she'll soon grow out of it,' Anstey murmured, more from hope than conviction.

'I'm sure she will,' Hazel agreed, but added reluctantly, 'I'm afraid Kenneth's—hmm—making noises about having a word with the landlord. I'm sorry,' she apologised. 'For myself, I'll be sorry too if you have to look for a new flat, but . . .'

'If Joanna isn't here by the morning, I stand to be looking for a new job before I start looking for a new flat,' Anstey butted in. And, with enough on her mind without the added threat of being evicted, she asked, 'Have you time for a cup of tea?'

'Love one,' Hazel accepted enthusiastically, more from the hope of still being there when Rosie awakened, Anstey guessed, than because she was dying of thirst. 'Why do you stand to be looking for a new job?'

Over the tea she told Hazel everything that she had not worked out for herself. And, thinking it out as she went along, Anstey told her that she would definitely have to have tomorrow off if Joanna did not appear. 'I shall have to spend the day searching for a baby-minder.' Anstey reached the only logical conclusion she could see.

'You can't do *that*!' Hazel declared, immediately alarmed. 'You can't leave Rosie with just *anybody*!'

Anstey too hated the very idea. 'What else can I do? I *have* to work,' she stated. Not to put too fine a point on it, she was as near flat-broke now as she was ever likely to be. Never had she suspected that infants were such a drain on the resources! With only one salary coming in now that Joanna had resigned her job, it was a constant headache to hang on until pay day.

'But a baby-minder—a highly recommended one,' Hazel inserted, 'will cost the earth.'

Anstey inwardly groaned at the prospect of another hefty chunk having to be found out of her monthly pay cheque. But, agreeing with Hazel that nothing but a highly recommended baby-minder would do, she sighed as she added in vain, 'If only my parents lived anywhere but in Long Kinnington, I'd take Rosie to my mother. She loves children, but . . .'

'But your mother lives right next door to Joanna's mother,' Hazel caught on, having over the last few years learned something of the background of the two friends. She also knew that Joanna felt it imperative that her down-trodden mother should not know about the baby.

'Exactly,' said Anstey. 'Joanna's stepfather would never cease to crow if he heard so much as a whisper about Rosie. My mother's a darling,' she went on, 'but I've been so afraid she might one day slip up and let something out that I've not breathed a word to her about Joanna's baby.'

'You couldn't very well take Rosie to her without a word of explanation of where she came from or whose child she is,' Hazel agreed. 'Besides . . .' suddenly, she stopped, 'I've just thought,' she cried, and started to smile, 'why can't *I* look after her!'

Astonished, Anstey stared. 'You!' she exclaimed, such a possibility never having occurred to her.

'I wouldn't charge you anything. Oh, do let me,' Hazel begged eagerly, and was so taken with the idea that Anstey was half-way to thinking it a splendid solution—until she remembered Hazel's husband.

'Kenneth,' she said, and as the light went out of Hazel's eyes, she did not have to say more.

'Oh—crumbs,' Hazel muttered, and looked thoroughly down cast. Suddenly, though, she brightened. 'Kenneth leaves for work before you,' she said quietly. 'Also, he comes home after you.'

'You wouldn't?' Anstey gasped, and realised that Hazel's loyalty to her husband was straining at the leash when she replied,

'Joanna might be back tomorrow. I needn't tell him—not for just one day.'

That one day had stretched into one week, and then two, with still no sign of Joanna. And while the baby continued to thrive, and Hazel had never looked more content, Anstey was growing more and more anxious.

After nights spent walking the floor with Rosie—about the only thing which seemed to keep her quiet—Anstey would be awakened in the early morning by another release of energy from the fractious infant. The fact that, as a result of her lack of sleep, her work at Elton Diesel was suffering was the least of her worries. For the longer Joanna stayed away, the larger her problems grew.

When one day her mother rang and in conversation asked after Joanna, Anstey was sorely struck by a wish to know where Joanna was. 'She's away—on holiday,' she invented on the spur of the moment.

'She's chosen some lovely weather for it,' Mrs Eldridge commented humorously. 'It's done nothing but rain this past month!'

'You haven't seen anything of her, then?'

'Whatever made you think she might ever return to Long Kinnington?' Anstey's mother asked in astonishment. 'It was the best day's work Joanna ever did when she packed her bags and, vowing never to return, got *permanently* away from her vile, self-righteous stepfather. Even if,' she added, 'I was more worried at the time that you decided to shake the dust of Long Kinnington off your boots to go to London with her.'

'I . . . You never said!' Anstey exclaimed. At nineteen she had thought it a marvellous idea to leave the village of her birth and try her wings in London. She had been so excited she had barely paused to consider that her parents might be upset that she wanted to leave her happy and comfortable home.

'Your father said not to raise any objection,' her mother replied. 'He said it was time to allow you to let go of the apron strings, and reminded me that—apart from the times when Jo used to disappear for weeks on end—the two of you had always been inseparable. He said he couldn't see how I'd ever thought that, when Joanna made that final break, you wouldn't want to go with her.'

'He's pretty smart, that father of mine,' Anstey said affectionately, reminded that in the old days it would be weeks before Joanna turned up to face the music.

'Why aren't you with Joanna this time?' Mrs Eldridge asked. 'I thought the two of you always spent your holidays together.'

'We're busy at work,' said Anstey off the top of her head.

'They can't spare you both away at the same time, I suppose,' her mother observed, aware that she and Joanna had worked for the same company, but unaware that Joanna had left some months previously. 'Talking of holidays,' she went on drily, 'you *do* know that you don't need a passport to pay a visit to Long Kinnington?'

Smitten with guilt that she hadn't paid her parents a visit since Rosie was born, Anstey excused, 'It's a bit hectic my way of the world just now,' that statement not covering a quarter of it.

'Well, don't let them work you too hard,' her mother replied, seeming to believe that she was putting in hours of overtime.

'I won't,' said Anstey, with more guilt on her conscience.

She came away from the phone, realising that she must have been supremely optimistic to think Joanna would be back within a few days. Even without her mother reminding her of her friend's track record, Joanna herself had said that the way she felt she would need a year to think Lester out of her system. True, it had been said half in jest, but, remembering how heart-and-soul in love Joanna had been, Anstey could only hope and pray that it wouldn't take that long.

Joanna had been gone three weeks when calamity struck. Anstey hurried home from her office, thanking her lucky stars for Hazel. The rate Rosie was growing she would very soon need a new three of everything in a larger size, but with the cost of baby clothes so prohibitive, it made employing the services of a professional baby-minder way beyond her means.

Wondering when, if ever, she would be able to pay a baby-minder, Anstey turned into the street where she lived. She was just musing that by the time she had got herself straight Rosie would no doubt need yet another larger size in clothes when she suddenly stopped dead.

That was Kenneth's car! Oh, lord, the unthinkable had happened—he had arrived home early! Fearing to upset the arrangement, she had not asked Hazel if she had told her husband that she was looking after Rosie during the day. But as she neared the outside door, Anstey knew in her bones that he had been kept in ignorance.

Sensing trouble, she squared her shoulders as she entered the building. Her senses had not played her false, she discovered when she knocked on the door of the ground-floor flat. Kenneth—a near apoplectic Kenneth—violently pulled back the door, to let forth hot and strong. The gist of it all, as Anstey looked past him to a tearful-looking Hazel who held Rosie in protective fashion, was that he had never come across such blankety-blank underhandedness, and that first thing tomorrow he was going to report the brat's presence to their landlord.

'I'm—sorry,' Hazel whispered as she handed Rosie over. 'I w . . .'

'*You're* sorry!' Kenneth shouted, his face livid.

Anything else he had to say was mercifully shortened by Rosie, who in her tender lifetime had taken it upon herself to believe that when it came to yelling, yelling was her prerogative, and promptly gave forth. Anstey thought it politic to take her upstairs.

With her monthly income more vital than ever, Anstey was forced to ring her boss the next day to ask if she could take the remainder of her holiday entitlement.

'I've noticed of late that your mind doesn't appear to be with your job,' Mr Sallis replied, disgruntled. 'You *do* wish to continue to work for this company?' he asked pointedly, more interested in profit than in taking into account the four years she had put in with the firm.

'Of course,' Anstey answered, and although it went against the grain, because she *needed* the income more than she *wished* to stay in his employ, she tended a placatory, 'It's just that I've a few—domestic problems, at the moment.'

'Let us both hope that your domestic problems are soon resolved,' he replied, with underlying threat.

Anstey rarely lost her temper, but, 'Men!' she fumed as she put down the phone. Rebelliously, she lumped all men together—her boss with his pound-of-flesh mentality, Lester Quartermaine with his careless regard for his own child, and Frank Wyatt, Joanna's beastly stepfather, who made it impossible for either her or Joanna to ask for help from home.

There was no sign of rebellion in Anstey the following morning when, if she had not done so already, she

discovered that troubles never came singly. The postman
delivered an electricity bill of such enormous proportions
that she just could not believe it. Nor, she realised a short
time later, could she pay it. Her spirits were flattened, and
for a while all she could do was to stare at the demand and
ponder on the possibility of some mistake having been
made.

She surfaced later to realise that, since this summer had
to be the wettest summer on record, and with it being
essential that Rosie's bedding and clothing were daily
washed, dried and aired, mammoth quantities of manufac-
tured heat had been gobbled up. Added to that, it was
important, according to the baby books she'd read, that if a
baby were to flourish, the surrounding temperature must
be maintained at a constant level. Where she and Joanna
might only switch on the heating if the evening turned
chilly, since the arrival of Rosie, the heating had never
been turned off!

By nightfall Anstey was at her wits' end. Certain that
yesterday Kenneth would have reported a baby in
residence in the first-floor flat, she reckoned that all she
needed now was to receive an eviction notice in tomorrow's
post.

A stiffness in her left arm brought Anstey to an
awareness that she had drifted off into a brown study of all
that had happened, and that she had been sitting with
Rosie crooked in her left arm for ages.

Rosie whimpered as she adjusted her position, but did not
awaken. What did awaken, though, was something in
Anstey. She had experienced a flicker of anger, of rebellion,
two days before. But, as she looked down at the defenceless
and totally dependent bundle in her arms, the slow fuse of
her anger was ignited. Alight suddenly, that flame would
not dim until she had taken some positive action.

She and Joanna thought alike in many ways, and they both had a high degree of pride. But while Anstey went along with her when Joanna's pride had decreed that her stepfather should not know the smallest cause to crow, 'I knew it, I said you'd come to a bad end,' Anstey discovered that pride concerning Lester Quartermaine was another matter.

Knowing her friend well, she was aware that when Joanna had got herself sorted out, her pride would see her wanting nothing from Lester for the child he had disowned. But he *was* the child's father, and—dammit—enough was enough. The least he could do was to pay something towards his child's upkeep.

Fear of waking Rosie prevented Anstey from going to the telephone right there and then. And when Rosie was awake she cried solidly until she had been fed. When finally she was settled in her cot, it was too late to ring Lester. But rebellion took a firmer and firmer hold when, through the night, between snatched hours of sleep, Anstey walked the floor with the baby.

She rang Lester Quartermaine's number early the next morning, but did not get any reply. Twice that day she went with Rosie to his address. He was not in. On the second occasion, she pushed a note through his letterbox asking him to phone her urgently.

The only use her phone had that evening was when she dialled his number, for Lester never rang her.

During her floor-walking excursions that night, Anstey racked her brains to try to remember if Joanna had said where Lester now worked. She was made more angry by the fact that he had ignored her urgent note, and that made her more determined to contact him, even if it meant she had to ring him at his place of work.

Although she couldn't remember where he worked, she

could remember many other things about him. Thinking
back, recalling how she had quite liked him until he had
treated Joanna so shabbily, Anstey remembered that he
hadn't had it too easy just lately either. When his elder
brother had so heartlessly got rid of him during some
rationalisation scheme or other at Quartermaine Holdings,
Lester had set up his own business. That business had folded
before Lester had it off the ground. Even his mother had
taken against him over something at one time, Anstey
recalled Joanna once telling her. Although, since Cale was
his mother's favourite, Lester probably wasn't given as
much rope as his brother.

Realising that she was starting to feel sorry for Lester,
Anstey hardened her heart. Feeling sorry for him was not
going to help pay the electricity bill, nor assist in paying for
the services of a baby-minder.

On Monday, Anstey's rebellion was spurred on by a
letter from her landlord. 'Thank you, Kenneth,' she
muttered, as she read how it had come to her landlord's ears
that the flat now housed a baby. The letter sternly
reminded her of the terms of her lease, and politely asked
for her comments.

At nine o'clock she rang Elton Diesel and by then cared
not if she had to lie her head off as she told Mr Sallis that she
had gone down with 'flu. Under the pretext of a coughing
bout, she rang off before he could request that she supply
him with a note from her doctor.

With a week of the same trauma stretching before her—
with no positive action having been taken—Anstey sat
down to think. Figuratively speaking, she had worn her
finger out dialling Lester's number, all to no avail, for he
was never in. Nor had she been able to come up with the
name of the firm he worked for. The prospect of having to
ring Elton Diesel again next Monday with the invention of

some fresh ailment was enough to make Anstey think hard.

Within fifteen minutes, her pretty chin set at a stubborn angle, she knew just what she was going to do. To seek help from her family, or Joanna's family, was definitely out. But—what about Lester's family? Confound it, Rosie was a Quartermaine—let them jolly well help!

Two minutes later she was on the line to Quartermaine Holdings. 'I'd like to speak to Mr Quartermaine, please,' she requested.

'Ringing for you.' Anstey grew hopeful.

'Mr Quartermaine's secretary,' said a different voice.

'Oh, good morning,' said Anstey brightly. 'I'd like to speak with Mr Quartermaine.'

She came away from the phone of the view that it would be easier to get to speak to the Russian premier than to get past Cale Quartermaine's secretary. Her call had been efficiently, if politely, blocked. Even her, 'It's a very personal matter,' had not got her past the charming but steel-plated Miss Impney.

'If you'd like to leave your name, address and telephone number, I'll advise Mr Quartermaine of your wish to contact him most urgently,' Miss Impney had replied when, refusing to give more details, Anstey had told her that the matter was most urgent.

Half an hour later, sitting waiting for the phone to ring, Anstey began to seethe that Cale Quartermaine had not rung back. She was starting to grow angry at being treated as if she was just one of a long line of females who regularly rang him under the guise of their business with him being very personal and most urgent, and an hour later her fury peaked.

At twelve-thirty, with Rosie in her arms, she entered the plush offices of Quartermaine Holdings. There were two receptionists on duty, but both were engaged with immaculately attired callers. Anstey went smartly to the lift. She pressed any button at random, and the lift reacted. Stepping out at the fifth floor, she adopted a lost look and addressed the first person she saw.

'I was directed to Mr Quartermaine's office, but . . .'

'You want the top floor,' answered the greying-haired lady, who appeared more interested in smiling at Rosie than in wondering what their business was.

Anstey thanked her, and stepped back into the lift. There was no one to be seen on the top floor, but it was a small matter to open any one of the doors in the corridor and to pop her head round.

'Mr Quartermaine's office?' she queried of the busy-looking executive who looked up.

'Last door on the right.'

'Thank you,' she smiled.

The last door on the right yielded an office occupied not by the male she had hoped to see, but a fortyish person of the female gender.

'Miss Impney?' Anstey enquired.

'How can I help you?' asked Miss Impney, warily eyeing the baby in Anstey's arms as if she considered her a time-bomb.

'I . . .' It was as far as she got. Used to admiration from any and every passer-by, Rosie took a dislike to being inspected in such an adverse manner, and suddenly took it into her head to tell the whole world of her existence.

'My goodness!' Miss Impney exclaimed above the din. 'How can such a tiny being create so much noise?'

'She gets lots of practice,' Anstey replied drily, and had bent her head to try to quieten the infant when the sudden sound of the other door in the room being angrily thrust open caused her to look up.

An all too obviously irritated man strode into the room,

halting when he saw them to demand, 'What the hell's going on?'

Hearing a voice louder than hers caused Rosie to stop yelling for a few seconds. In those few seconds Anstey knew that, quite definitely, this was the man she was here to see. Even though this man was the entire opposite of Lester in every way—tall where Lester was stocky, dark-haired where Lester was fair, grey-eyed where Lester's were blue—she just knew that this authoritative-looking man was Lester's brother. The biggest difference between them was that, whereas Lester's mouth held a trace of weakness, in this man's firm and well-shaped mouth, of weakness Anstey could see no sign.

Lester had said that his brother was seven years older than himself, which would make Cale Quartermaine thirty-seven. Suddenly though, as cold grey eyes pierced hers, and she realised that he was waiting, none too patiently, for an answer to his question of 'What the hell's going on?' Anstey decided that it had been folly to spend some of her precious resources on a taxi ride across London. She could have saved herself the expense, because she was going to get no help from Cale Quartermaine—she knew that before she started.

CHAPTER TWO

'WELL?' Cale Quartermaine demanded, as Rosie started off again, this time in search of louder decibels.

Anstey had a speech prepared, but she was distracted by Rosie's noise, and opened with none of what she had ready. 'I thought,' she said, 'that it was about time you became acquainted with your niece.'

'My—niece?'

His amazement made Anstey realise at once that Lester had said nothing to him of Joanna. 'You are Mr Cale Quartermaine—Lester's brother?' she asked.

It could have been purely a disinclination on his part to compete with the yelling infant. But when all Cale Quartermaine did to acknowledge who he was was to give a curt nod, Anstey's preformed dislike of him was confirmed.

'Then allow me,' she said tartly, her chin tilting, her tone holding none of the pleasantness with which she had intended to explain the position to him, 'to introduce your niece, Miss Rosie Tresilla . . .' She got no further.

'Tresilla?' he questioned, and paused to send an impatient look to the still wailing Rosie. 'You'd better come into my office,' he said curtly, and was already on the move when Anstey, with Rosie's unabating noise, went to follow him. Swiftly he turned. 'Miss Impney,' he barked, 'take charge of—of that.' Having issued his orders, he disappeared inside his office.

Angered to hear Rosie being called 'that', Anstey decided that the baby would stay with her throughout whatever type of discussion went on. Common sense, though, suddenly reared its head. Cale Quartermaine appeared an impatient and easily irritated man. The interview could only go from bad to worse if they had to yell over the top of Rosie's vociferations the whole time.

'She likes to be walked up and down,' Anstey said apologetically as she placed the aggrieved bundle into the arms of an all at once terrified-looking Miss Impney.

Cale Quartermaine was standing impatiently waiting when Anstey went in and closed the door. She noted the shrewd look about him as he drew a chair up to his huge desk and told her abruptly, 'Take a seat.'

Striving to keep calm, she sat down and had a few moments in which to regain some of her scattered composure while he went and took his seat on the opposite side of the desk. With the huge desk between them like some demarcation line, she opened her mouth. But it was he who spoke first.

'I had no idea,' he clipped, 'that my brother had got himself a wife.'

'Your brother,' Anstey told him bluntly, 'has not got himself a wife. He . . .'

'Well, it's for sure he damn well knows you—intimately,' he cut in disagreeably, as he took her reply on board.

Anstey's dislike of him went up another notch. It was her intention then to tell him that, although of course she knew Lester, the baby was not hers. That intention, though, was somehow lost.

'You mean because of the baby?'

She hadn't thought of it before, but it had suddenly dawned on her that Cale Quartermaine, as hard as she had thought him, could easily want more proof that the baby was Lester's than just her saying so.

'I mean because of the child's second name,' he replied shortly. 'Tresilla is my mother's middle name. It's a family name on her side which—for no known reason—is never broadcast, but which is always given as a middle name to any female descendant. Clearly,' he stated, 'your relationship with my brother is a close one.'

'Ah,' Anstey murmured, only then understanding why, no matter what other names Joanna had thought of, Tresilla had been settled as a girl-child's middle name from the beginning.

'So,' Cale Quartermaine, plainly a busy man, went on, 'having got that out of the way, we come to the reason for your visit.'

Cold grey eyes again pierced hers and, as clearly as if he had said it, she knew that he was thinking that she was there for a handout. She swallowed hard on pride, and if there had been only herself to consider, she would have got up right then and walked out. But she could not afford such luxury. Nor, she discovered, although it was the only reason she was there, could she ask him for money.

'I'm trying,' she said as calmly as she could, 'to trace your brother.'

A dark frown appeared on his face. 'He's deserted you?' he asked sharply.

'Not me,' Anstey retorted, 'my friend.'

'Your friend?' It became apparent then that the head of Quartermaine Holdings cared not one whit for talking in riddles. 'What the hell sort of a mess has he got himself into this time?' he erupted disagreeably. 'Good God!' he exploded in utter disgust. 'Are you saying that he lived with two of you at the same time?'

'No, I'm not!' Anstey said heatedly, as disgusted as him by the very thought. 'And Lester lived with neither of us. He and Joanna . . .' She broke off, and took a grip on herself. 'My name,' she said as calmly as she could, 'is Anstey Eldridge. I share a flat with my very good friend, Joanna Keeble. Joanna and Lester are—were . . .' she broke off to gather more calm, '. . . were in love. Only, when—

when Lester knew that Rosie was—was on the way, he didn't care much for the idea.'

'He ducked out when he knew he was to be a father?' Cale Quartermaine questioned tersely.

'Not straight away,' Anstey replied. 'But Joanna hasn't seen anything of him for months now.'

A steely look entered the eyes of the man opposite her. 'Leaving aside the fact that I'm wondering why you're here—and not your *friend*,' he said coolly, giving her a vivid impression that he had no belief any such friend existed, 'carry on with your—tale.'

Again Anstey had to quell the impulse to get up and leave. 'My friend—Joanna,' she said tartly, 'is not here, because she has gone away.'

'She left—without her baby?' There was so much scepticism in his question that, for the first time in her life, Anstey felt like hitting a man.

'Joanna left her baby with a neighbour until I arrived home,' she began to explain with what civility she had remaining. 'When Lester denied parenthood . . .'

'He says he's not the father?' The sudden stilled look of him told Anstey that he had latched on to what she had just said, and that, as his brother had disclaimed fatherhood of Rosie, Cale Quartermaine was getting ready to deny that he was Rosie's uncle.

'He *is* the father!' Anstey said in sudden fury. 'He knows it, and I know it, just as anyone who knew Joanna would know it too! Lester,' she stormed on angrily with a toss of her short blonde hair, 'told her it was either an abortion or him. Joanna thought he would change his mind, but she saw less and less of him while she was pregnant, and he wouldn't even go to see her when she was in hospital. She rang him when she wanted him named as Rosie's father on her full birth certificate, he refused, and Joanna was upset, and had to go away.' Having run out of steam, Anstey sat and glared across the desk. Cale Quartermaine was totally unmoved.

'So—whose name does the child have?'

'She's a Quartermaine—much good will it do her,' Anstey snapped, getting personal when she hadn't intended to. Again she strove for calm. 'She has been registered in the name Rosie Tresilla Quartermaine—as is her right.'

The hard grey-eyed man nodded, though whether in confirmation that he agreed she could not tell. But she was made fiercely angry when, giving her the impression that he thought Joanna was someone she had just dreamed up for the benefit of her 'tale', he summed up, 'So—my brother sires an offspring, and deserts both mother and child. Mother of said child then deserts her own child and—via a neighbour—leaves child with a "friend". I confess, Miss—er—Eldridge, I'm still a shade in the dark about what you expect me to do about it. But, tell me, do you have other children you look after when their parents desert them, or . . .'

'I don't,' Anstey said between her teeth, 'have other children; I happen to have a job at Elton Diesel. A job which I'm hoping still to have if my employer doesn't dismiss me for absenteeism on account of my looking after Rosie. And as for what I expect you to do about it—you've made it perfectly plain that I can expect nothing from you. It matters nothing to you,' she said as, more angry than ever, she left her chair, 'that because of your flesh and blood out there, I have an electricity bill I can't pay and that before long my electricity supply will be cut off.' Cale Quartermaine's getting to his feet too threw her for a second, although she thought his action was more to show that he thought this intrusion into his day was over than from any attempt to show her courtesy. 'That,' she charged on, 'because children are not allowed where I live, I stand to be evicted any day.'

'You're behind with your rent too, no doubt,' he cut in, plainly disliking her as much as she disliked him.

'Not yet,' she retorted. 'But at the rate your niece is growing, she'll soon outgrow her clothes. The money for the next size will have to be found from somewhere.'

'Which brings us to the crux of why you're here—money!'

Her pride was instantly out in force. 'I wouldn't touch a penny of your money!' she spat as he took a few aggressive steps round his desk and came closer.

'Not much, you wouldn't,' he said loftily, and challenged harshly, 'Isn't it the truth that, knowing Lester's connections were not so impoverished, you deliberately got yourself pregnant thinking to guarantee yourself a meal ticket for life.'

The heated words, 'The baby's not mine!' had left Anstey before the awful import of what he had just said fully sank in. Then, because she was so close to Joanna who had given herself to Lester only from love, it felt as though he had said such a terrible thing directly to her dear friend. Anstey experienced such an uprush of infuriated feeling that nothing would do but that she let it have its way. With the accompanying words, 'Why, you evil-minded swine . . .!' her right hand swung through the air, and she struck Cale Quartermaine a blow of such force that it would not have surprised her if she had broken her wrist.

His poleaxed expression as his head jerked back was quickly followed by a look of such malevolence that Anstey immediately realised that she had better remove herself—smartish. She was wasting her time in staying to try to seek help from him, anyway. Fearing, when Cale Quartermaine took an ominous step forwards, that she might well receive some of her own medicine, Anstey wasted not another word on him. In swift flight she left his office, swooped Rosie up from Miss Impney in her stride, and hastily departed.

It took Anstey some time to accept that, when pushed, she had a temper that was as spirited as anyone else's. By the next morning, though, she was still not regretting that she, who had never struck a blow in her life, had very nearly knocked Cale Quartermaine's head off his shoulders. About that she was entirely unrepentant. What she did regret, however, was that she had not first found out from him where Lester worked.

Laden down with depressing worries, she began to wish that she had never left her comfortable and trouble-free home in Long Kinnington. A moment later she was ashamed. As she had said to Joanna, what were friends for? She'd be a fine sort of fair-weather friend if she started to have regrets as soon as the going got tough.

She ignored the small voice that said 'tough' was an understatement for the pickle she was in. Instead, she made herself think back to her eagerness to accompany Joanna when her friend, worn down by constant strife and misery from her bullying stepfather, had decided to get out, this time never to go back.

It hadn't been easy for Joanna. Frank Wyatt, realising that his whipping post would be gone when she decamped, had been more verbally abusive to her than ever in the week leading up to her departure. Joanna had been in tears when she'd confided how he'd raged on for hours about how she would come to no good, and how she would end up living a loose life. Sorely distressed on her behalf, Anstey had comforted her, saying, 'We'll show him.' Joanna had gradually brightened, and it was then that they'd made their pact. They would go to London, find a flat—where no man would stay overnight—and they would carve out brilliant careers for themselves. They would both show Frank Wyatt!

Some of it had worked. They had come to London and, after much searching, they had found a flat. No man had stayed in their flat overnight either, although, in all honesty, neither of them had gone so overboard for any of their dates that they'd found any difficulty in showing them the door.

As for carving out brilliant careers, though, they had found living and fending for themselves in London expensive, and could not afford the luxury of waiting for the right sort of job. The first job they'd been offered together was in the typing pool at Elton Diesel. It was mundane work, but the need for job security, which in turn meant financial security, made them stick it out for two years, when around the same time they were both promoted to secretarial status.

Some time later, Joanna had met Lester Quartermaine, and had fallen completely and utterly in love with him. It was then that their pact not to have men stay overnight became strained. One Sunday evening Anstey returned from a weekend visit to her parents to learn that their pact had been broken.

'Lester stayed last night,' Joanna, always straight with her, had confessed. As she confessed too, 'I wish, Anstey, I could say that I'm sorry, but I'm not.' And while Anstey had stared at the shine in her friend's eyes, and acknowledged the way in which Joanna had blossomed since she had known Lester, Joanna had added, 'Lester has asked me to go away with him next weekend. I love him so much, Anstey—nothing else matters but him—I shall have to go.'

'Of course you will, love,' Anstey had said quietly, never having been in love and slightly in awe of the emotion which had put such a light in Joanna's eyes and had her forgetful of everything, the gibes and barbs of her stepfather included.

'Thank you—for understanding,' Joanna had smiled.

She'd kept on smiling too, and had blossomed even more,

and then—she had become pregnant.

Anstey shook herself out of her reverie, but she was saddened that the love which had so totally consumed Joanna had come to such a disastrous end. It wasn't fair. Joanna had been through a miserable adolescence at home, and she had never hurt a soul in her whole life—it just wasn't fair.

Her feelings and sensitivities all for Joanna, Anstey remembered the way Cale Quartermaine had accused Joanna, albeit through her, of deliberately getting herself pregnant in order to ensure she had a meal ticket for life. What a swine of a man he was! she thought, and experienced such an uprush of anger that were Cale Quartermaine suddenly to appear, she would have hit him again.

Anstey calmed down, though she felt quite regretful that the chance to have a second swipe at another of the planet's most vile inhabitants was not to be. It went without saying that she was never going to see him again. In that thought, though, Anstey discovered she was wrong.

She had just settled Rosie down after an early evening feeding session that had taken all of an hour when there was an unexpected knock at her door. She realised immediately that it wouldn't be Hazel—not while Kenneth was at home. What if it was their landlord, though, come in person for a reply to his letter?

Oh, grief! Anstey took a quick look round the sittting-room and quailed. Apart from a clothes horse literally festooned with baby garments, evidence of a baby in residence was everywhere!

The knock came again, louder this time. Afraid that another louder knock might awaken Rosie, when it would take another hour to get her settled, Anstey hurried to the door.

She opened the door the merest crack, and relief flooded

her to see that it was not her landlord. Her feeling of relief, however, was swiftly replaced by one of anger. For the dark-suited, tall, dark-haired man who stood unsmiling looking down at her reminded her just why she had hit him. She pulled the door open a little wider, uncaring of the proof behind her of a baby living there.

'To what do I owe this inauspicious pleasure?' she asked sourly.

Cale Quartermaine eyed her hostilely for about two seconds. But, while she read in his expression that he was about to issue a curt 'Damn you' and depart, he surprised her by doing nothing of the kind.

'We need to talk,' he said shortly. And when she showed no inclination to invite him in, he asked, 'Do you want to bring your chair out here?'

It was on the tip of her tongue to tell him that she had heard him say more than enough, but Kenneth Davies emerging from his flat and looking up put her off.

'Come in—if you must,' she found herself offering ungraciously, and immediately Cale Quartermaine was in her flat, she wanted him out again. Suddenly she felt threatened. It might well have been that, with him inside, an already shrinking flat seemed totally overcrowded. But, either from some maternalistic urge to protect Rosie, or a need to gather some composure, Anstey mumbled, 'Just a minute, I want to check on Rosie.'

She had left him in the sitting-room, and was bent over the baby and about to replace the kicked-off covers when she was suddenly startled to find that Cale Quartermaine had followed her. She was more mesmerised than startled, however, when with an infinitely gentle touch he reached down and examined where the second and third toes on Rosie's right foot were joined together in webbed fashion almost to the top.

Bemused that such a broad-shouldered, athletic-looking

man could have such gentleness—for, miraculously, Rosie did not so much as stir—Anstey continued to stare at him.

'She's inherited the Yoxhall toes,' he murmured, and released Rosie's chubby foot and stood back while Anstey covered her over.

'Yoxhall?' she queried.

'My mother's family,' he replied, adding, a shade sharply, 'Didn't my brother tell you that when he confided about the family name Tresilla?'

'Joanna was the one he confided in, not me,' she erupted, her sharp tone disturbing Rosie more than Cale Quartermaine's, so that she whimpered in her sleep.

Anstey gave him a 'Now see what you've done' look, and, taking the hint, he went to wait in the other room.

Fortunately Rosie, after making her protest known, slumbered on. Anstey stayed with her for a few more minutes just to make sure, and then returned to the sitting-room.

'I would have preferred that you answered my urgent phone call of yesterday morning, rather than coming to my home in person.' She jumped into battle straight away. For her pains all she received was a cold-eyed stare. 'I assume,' she went on belligerently, 'that it was your secretary who gave you my address. Or,' she said quickly, her belligerence falling away as a sudden thought came to her, 'did Lester tell you where . . .'

'It's quite some time since I last saw my brother,' Cale Quartermaine cut her off.

That figured, Anstey realised. A man who could so ruthlessly end his brother's career would not have the sentiment to find out how he had fared since, or want to see him from any feeling of brotherly love.

'But you do know where he works?' she pressed, determined suddenly not to make the same mistake she had made yesterday when she had left Quartermaine Holdings without that piece of information. 'As I told you, I'm trying to trace him. I've rung his flat, and called round several times, only he's never in. So if you could tell me where he works, I could . . .'

'To the best of my knowledge,' Cale Quartermaine sliced her off, 'he doesn't.'

'Work, you mean?' He nodded, and Anstey felt defeated. Quickly, though, she pulled herself together. 'Well—thank you for calling,' she said primly, and was half-way to the door when he halted her.

'Are you always such a little hothead?' he asked.

'Me!' she turned to exclaim, hothead being the last thing she would have called herself. Near-demented with worry, maybe—but hothead!

'You,' he stated briefly. 'I've said we need to have a discussion.' He had no need to add that he did not intend to leave until he had said his piece, it was all there in his authoritative stance.

Anstey had no intention of bowing to his authority. 'What brought this on?' she asked tartly. 'Yesterday, you weren't interested in anything I had to say!'

'Yesterday,' he countered tersely, 'you took a violent swipe at me. If furious, I was at the same time rendered speechless. I never knew,' he muttered, 'that such a slender female could pack such a wallop!'

If Anstey hadn't known better, she would have thought his tone held a trace of humour. 'You deserved it,' she snapped. 'Joanna is the sweetest, kindest person. She wanted her baby because she loved Lester. She just doesn't think the way you suggested. I know her. I've known her all my life.'

'This Joanna—she does exist?'

'Of course she exists,' Anstey said shortly, 'I've told y . . .'

'And the child—Rosie—she's Joanna's child?'

'Joanna's and Lester's,' Anstey replied, and had the fact

of two of Rosie's toes to thank that Cale Quartermaine said,

'There's no mistake about who her father is. You—your friend . . .' he began, but Anstey had a feeling that he still did not believe that Joanna existed, and suddenly, she had remembered something.

Without word or excuse, she left him to dart noiselessly into the bedroom. She returned carrying a framed photograph that had stood on a table between their two beds, facing Joanna's bed. Still without a word, she handed the picture to him.

Silently he studied the enlarged snapshot of Joanna and Lester standing with their arms entwined, their love and happiness in each other there for all the world to see.

'Joanna?' Cale Quartermaine clipped as he handed the picture back. Anstey nodded, and he went on, 'Has she seen him or had any communication from him since her baby was born?'

'They've spoken on the phone—that's all,' Anstey replied.

'Which means she hasn't received any maintenance payment from him?'

'Joanna would never ask him for money, I know that,' Anstey said, but she felt uncomfortable when honesty forced her to add, 'Just as I know that I'm going against what she would want by trying to contact him. But until she returns and we can get something worked out—I can't think what else to do.'

'It's a mess,' Cale Quartermaine agreed—about the only thing they did agree on. 'But, for a start, I'll settle any unpaid bills. If you'll hand over . . .'

Immediately Anstey felt hot under the collar. 'Why should you settle anything?' she asked, pride and the memory of telling him that she wouldn't touch a penny of his money making her argumentative. 'The last time I saw you, you didn't want to know . . .'

'The last time I saw *you*,' he cut in, 'you reminded me that the infant also happens to be my flesh and blood. I may not like the circumstances,' he continued, 'but I find I just cannot simply turn my back on that fact.'

Anstey was surprised, to say the least; her eyes widened. The flesh-and-blood factor hadn't bothered him when he'd wanted his brother out of his firm!

'Incredible colour,' he muttered, as he looked into eyes that were so dark a blue as to appear navy. Abruptly though, as if he regretted the personal utterance, he went on—to her astonishment—'You'll have to give up your job, of course. It's . . .'

'Give up my job?' Anstey exclaimed incredulously, taking the greatest exception to what he had said, and taking exception also to being ordered around by the bossy arrogant brute.

'Your job means so much to you?' questioned Cale Quartermaine curtly, observing that his suggestion had not gone down so well.

'Not so much,' her innate honesty made her answer. 'As secretarial work goes, I suppose it's fairly run-of-the-mill. But that's not the point,' she said shortly. 'I need that job. More than ever now, I need to bring in some kind of an income. Besides,' she added when she realised that he seemed unimpressed by her argument, 'what do I do for a job when Joanna returns?'

'From what you've said, you've no idea when she'll return,' he replied bluntly. 'You've also said that you stand to be dismissed for absenteeism anyway,' he reminded her, when she would rather he hadn't. 'You'll have to admit,' he argued logically, 'that you can't keep on with your job and, at the same time, look after the infant.'

'Quite obviously,' Anstey countered, 'you've never heard of the services of a baby-minder.'

'A baby-minder!' he repeated, and frowned so darkly

that Anstey knew he cared not one little bit for the idea of her farming his niece out to strangers during the day. She didn't like the idea either but, made to feel guilty and as though she had just suggested something detrimental to the baby's wellbeing, she bridled.

'If you don't like the idea,' she gibed, not meaning a word of it, 'you could always take a turn in looking after Rosie.'

'Good God!' he exclaimed. 'You're not seriously suggesting that *I* should house the child!'

That he looked as appalled as he sounded angered Anstey. The fact that his sense of responsibility towards his brother's child soon disintegrated when he was faced with the prospect of having to do more than dip into his wallet stirred her to more belligerence.

'Aside from the fact that I wouldn't leave a pet frog in your care,' she erupted snappily, 'in these days of role-sharing—why shouldn't you?'

Cale Quartermaine favoured her with a hostile look, his glance leaving her to take in the cluttered-up sitting-room. 'My apartment, I'll grant, is large,' he informed her coldly. 'But it's high up, and is no more a suitable place to rear a child than this—this cubby-hole.'

'Thank you,' Anstey muttered, offended to hear his description of what had been an adequate-sized flat before Rosie's arrival. But all at once she felt near to the end of her tether. The whole situation seemed to lurch from one nightmare to another. 'We won't even have this cubby-hole, as you so delightfully term it,' she said wearily, her anger gone, 'if the tenant downstairs gets his way and we're evicted for having a baby here.'

'You've heard from your landlord?' asked Cale Quartermaine, his eyes on her suddenly defeated expression.

Anstey nodded. 'He's waiting for my reply to his question—do you have a baby in the flat?' Her voice was wistful when she added, 'If only my mother didn't live next door to Joanna's; then at least I'd have some breathing space in which to fob off my landlord, and be able to carry on my job without using an outside baby-minder.'

'You're suggesting taking the infant to your mother?'

'That's exactly what I'm *not* suggesting,' Anstey replied. And somehow, she found herself giving him a brief outline of what a dreadful man Joanna's stepfather was. 'Because of the misery he'll cause her mother, Joanna has decided that it's best Mrs Wyatt knows nothing of her grandchild. For that reason,' she went on to explain, 'bearing in mind that not only Joanna's mother but all of Long Kinnington will ask questions, I can't take Rosie to my mother.'

'Your mother—she'll know the infant isn't yours?'

'I couldn't lie to her about a thing like that!' Anstey exclaimed, astounded. And lest his suggestion came from any lingering doubt that it was she and not Joanna who had given Rosie birth, she added, 'Apart from anything else, my visits to my parents have been frequent enough for my mother to observe that my figure has never changed shape. But in any case,' she went on to exclaim, 'have you no idea of the utter joy a mother knows when presented with her *first grandchild*? Once my mother was over the shock,' she warmed to her theme, 'she'd be so thrilled, she'd be ready to forgive me anything—were I to do anything so underhand as make her believe that Rosie was mine.'

The sudden alert look in Cale Quartermaine's eyes made Anstey aware that she had given him food for thought, and that his brain cogs were working overtime. Though as she was about to repeat swiftly that there was no way she was going to pass Rosie off to her mother as hers, he got in first.

'You're sure—about a mother's reception to her first grandchild?' he pressed seriously.

'Positive,' she answered. 'A couple of women at Elton Diesel commiserate endlessly with each other over the way *their* mothers are so besotted with their grandchildren they

let them get away with murder. But,' she added quickly, to
knock on the head any idea he might still have of
misleading her parent, 'I am not taking Rosie to my
mother, or making any futile attempt to convince her that
Rosie is her granddaughter.'

Seconds passed when, as though arrested by the sparks
flashing in her eyes, Cale Quartermaine said not a word.
Then, quite clearly, he said, 'I'm not asking you to take the
infant to any make-believe grandmother.' He paused, then
added, 'We'll take her to her rightful grandmother.'

Her eyes saucer-wide, Anstey stared at him. 'No way!'
she told him forthrightly as she started to recover. 'Joanna
would hit the roof if I took Rosie to her mother in Suffolk!'

'Which is why we won't take her there. I propose,' said
Cale Quartermaine, his tone brooking no refusal, 'to take
the infant to her paternal grandmother—in Hampshire.'

CHAPTER THREE

HAD she really agreed to that impossible man's suggestion? Busy with her chores on Wednesday morning, Anstey found it more and more incredible that she had actually agreed to take Rosie to Hampshire! Had she really consented last night that on Saturday morning, being too busy before then, apparently, Cale Quartermaine should call to drive them to his mother's home?

Aware that she had indeed consented, Anstey went back over her conversation with him. She had not, she recalled, given in without protest to his cool, 'I propose to take the infant to her paternal grandmother—in Hampshire.'

'Now just a minute!' she had flared, winded, but not prepared to be brushed out of the way as if she had no say in the matter. 'I'm not so sure that I want Rosie to go to her grandmother.'

His arrogant look down his straight nose gave her the impression that he thought she was being tiresome merely for the sake of it. He was blunt too, when he coldly informed her, 'I've accepted that you can't go out to your job *and* stay at home to mind the baby. What I won't accept is that the child be pushed out to a baby-minder, even if you could afford one, which I suspect you can't. I'm fully prepared to pay all expenses incurred by that small scrap, but I've no intention whatsoever of paying baby-minder fees when that child has a grandmother who, according to you, will be thrilled at the sight of her first grandchild.'

'But I didn't mean . . .'

'Had the circumstances of your friend's home-life been— more favourable,' he chopped her off as if she had not spoken, 'you'd have been ready to take the child to your mother, or, quite probably, her maternal grandmother. I see little difference,' he said loftily, 'which grandparent looks after the infant during her mother's absence.'

Anstey decided there and then that she hated logical-thinking men. There were emotions involved here!

'But I'm not sure that Joanna would want Lester's mother to know about her baby, any more than she wants her own mother to know,' she argued. 'She . . .'

'Joanna limited her options on the day she walked out and left you to manage as best you could,' Cale Quartermaine sliced in.

'I've told you all about that,' Anstey said heatedly. 'It was your brother's heartless treatment of her that . . . Oh, what's the use?' she said aggressively. 'You're as heartless as he is!'

'Whatever,' he shrugged, not even dented. 'You need help. I'm prepared to give that help.'

'But only if I do things your way!'

He did not deign to answer, but she knew, frustratedly, that it was he who called the tune. Dearly, then, she wanted to tell him that she could manage without his help. But— she faced the truth—she could not manage without somebody's help, and so far, he was the only one to come up with any scheme which might ensure she was back at her desk on Monday.

Even so, Anstey still did not like it, though, since anything she had found to say in opposition had been swept aside by precise logic, all she had left was to argue from the emotional aspect.

'What if your mother doesn't take to Rosie?'

'Her first grandchild?' he questioned, to make Anstey regret she had ever breathed a word about the utter joy a mother knows when presented with her first grandchild.

'Yes, but . . .' Stumped for a brief moment, Anstey soon

found fresh argument. 'What if it isn't convenient for your mother to have her? I mean,' she added hurriedly, as she did a quick mental calculation, 'Mrs Quartermaine must be in her sixties, and children can be exhausting at the . . .'

'My mother is sixty-five,' he cut her off, a habit he had which was starting to irk Anstey. 'And apart from other help in the house, the woman who took a turn in looking after both my brother and me when we were youngsters was widowed last year and has returned to her employ. Netty Lewis, I assure you, will be delighted to give a hand with the infant.'

My stars! Anstey thought, stunned, as it registered that, while she was recovering from his astonishing statement that he proposed to take Rosie to his mother, Cale Quartermaine had already got the 'i's dotted and the 't's crossed! He had left her with nothing to do but agree! That, too, niggled.

'You're not taking Rosie without me,' she said belligerently.

'I'm glad about that,' he answered, a suggestion of humour playing around his mouth. 'I confess, babies terrify me.'

A mental picture of Cale Quartermaine at his wits' end when, as he was trying to concentrate on his driving, Rosie starting yelling—and she would—made it tempting for Anstey to invent some reason why she couldn't accompany them.

'And I'm not leaving her with your mother if—if it doesn't feel right,' she stated flatly.

'Which is why I suggest you spend the weekend at Quiet Ways.' Cale Quartermaine took the wind from her sails. Quiet Ways, Anstey assumed, was the name of his mother's home—though it wouldn't be quiet much longer. When Rosie got there . . . 'I'll pick you up on Saturday. Can you be ready by ten?'

'No, I can't!' Anstey exclaimed, feeling breathless at the pace he was pushing her along, and glad to be able to put up some opposition. 'Rosie has to be bathed and fed. She won't finish her bottle until nearly eleven.'

'I'll make it eleven, then,' he said coolly.

She realised at that point that she had virtually agreed to go with him. But since her options were few, she had one last thing to say to him before he went.

'You understand, Mr Quartermaine,' she said, fixing him with a serious stare, 'that it might only be for a few days. At the most,' she qualified, 'a few weeks.' His glance settled on her earnest expression, and she continued solemnly, 'I promised Joanna I would keep her baby safe. She'll need her when she comes home.'

For an age, Cale Quartermaine looked into her deep blue eyes without comment. Then suddenly his mouth curved in a trace of a smile. 'I understand,' he said quietly, and still had that hint of a curve to his mouth when he checked his watch and said, 'Now, if you'll pass me all your unpaid accounts, I'll be on my way.'

Afterwards, Anstey thought it must have been that trace of a human smile on the man she had dubbed as heartless which was responsible for her forgetting that she was not going to touch a penny of his money.

'There's only one outstanding bill,' she had replied, finding the electricity account and handing it over. 'I'm sorry it's so large,' she had apologised, gabbling on to get over a pride-induced uncomfortable moment, 'only with the weather so awful, and Rosie's washing to dry, and the flat having to be kept at the same temperature . . .'

'We mustn't let my niece catch cold,' he'd cut her gabbling off. In the same action of putting the unpaid account into his wallet, he extracted and passed her a card with the comment, 'Should you need to contact me out of office hours,' and added as he walked to the door, 'Until Saturday, Miss Eldridge,' and left her.

Anstey admitted as she went to bed that Cale Quartermaine, without trying, had stirred in her a latent argumentative streak. So how come she had handed over that electricity bill without so much as a murmur? She remembered that trace of a smile she had seen on his mouth, and for all of a confused five seconds she was aghast at the thought that—was it his smile that had disarmed her?

By morning, Anstey was certain that Cale Quartermaine's smile had no power to affect her whatsoever. Any wisp of doubt, though, was quickly forgotten when she started to have doubts on another score. Had she really agreed to take Rosie to Hampshire? Was she doing the right thing?

By Saturday she had spent a deal of time in trying to see the situation with some of Cale Quartermaine's logic. When, at eleven on the dot, he arrived to pick them up, she had her priorities in order. If she was to keep her job, then she had to be in work on Monday. Her first priority, therefore, had to be that Rosie was looked after in her absence by some responsible and caring adult. Who, she asked, could there be who would be more responsible and caring than Rosie's own grandmother?

'I should have contacted Pickfords!' Cale Quartermaine remarked when he saw the mountain of luggage that was to go with them.

Anstey's lips gave a wayward quirk, but she controlled her smile before it could break. 'Your niece likes to change several times a day,' she murmured, and did a few last-minute jobs while he went up and down the stairs. She was waiting with Rosie in her arms when he returned from taking the last of the luggage, which included her weekend case, out to the car.

'I'll just lock up,' she told him and, remembering his confession of how babies terrified him, she was surprised when, as if about to slay some personal dragon, he muttered grimly,

'I'll carry the infant down the stairs.'

'You hold them this way up,' she mumbled, passing the baby over, but not expecting him to hear.

'Shut up, Miss Eldridge,' he said distinctly, and left her staring after him when, holding the baby gingerly, he went out.

Anstey was glad he could not see the smile that broke on her mouth. Abruptly she cancelled the smile. The strain's been too much for me, I'm going light-headed, she thought.

'I've harnessed the carry-cot to the back seat,' he informed her when she joined him beside an opulent-looking vehicle.

'That's thoughtful of you,' Anstey replied politely as she took the baby from him. 'But I think I'd better hang on to Rosie. She has the most unladylike way of screaming at the top of her lungs at any given moment. You'd only have to pull over for me to pick her up.'

'As you wish,' he said curtly, opening the front passenger door and assisting her in. 'Though in my view, it's a great mistake to overindulge a child.'

Pig! Anstey fumed, once more made instantly angry by the cold-hearted brute. 'Have you had many?' she asked waspishly, when he got in beside her.

'What?' he asked, mystified.

'Children,' she enlightened him. 'You sound as though you've had half a dozen.'

'I'm a bachelor, and intend to stay that way,' she was coldly informed.

'So's your brother,' Anstey said acidly. His chin jutting, Cale Quartermaine set the car in motion.

It was not a very good start. The first part of the journey was covered in grim silence. Then Rosie decided to liven things up. She yelled; Anstey crooned to her and tried to soothe her. Rosie did not want to know.

'My God!' Cale exclaimed. 'When does she stop?'

'She likes to be walked,' Anstey told him.

Immediately, he pulled into a lay-by. 'Then walk her,' he grunted.

'You—er—don't think I'm being overindulgent?' Anstey asked sweetly.

He gave her a speaking look, and then came round to open the passenger door. Anstey stepped out into the first sunshine of the summer and walked with the baby. When Rosie felt damp, she changed her and then walked up and down with her for a few minutes until Rosie, looking nothing short of angelic, succumbed to sleep. Anstey got back into the car, and the car was guided smoothly back on to the road.

It was then that she thought to ask the belated question, 'Your mother raised no—objection—when you told her about Rosie, Mr Quartermaine?'

He took his eyes momentarily from the road, and let his glance encompass both Anstey and the sound asleep babe. Then, looking to the front again, he quietly let fall, 'I didn't tell her about the baby.'

'You didn't tell . . .' Dumbfounded, Anstey stared at his strong profile.

'I phoned her, naturally, to tell her I was bringing a small surprise today, but . . .'

'Small surprise!' Anstey exploded.

'Shh—the baby,' warned Cale as Rosie gave a small cry in her sleep.

Anstey had to take a few deep breaths before she could speak with any sort of quiet control. 'You mean you haven't told her anything at all about the baby? That her *small surprise*,' she hissed, 'is Lester's child? Th-that,' she spluttered, 'it's your intention to leave Rosie with her when we return to London tomorrow!'

'Do calm down, Miss Eldridge,' he instructed her coolly. 'I thought it better to be there when my mother learns of her first grandchild. Add to that the fact that you've stated you will only leave the infant at Quiet Ways—if it feels right—and you'll see that I couldn't very well tell her I was bringing her granddaughter to stay in her care for a short while, when there's a small question mark over whether I shall have to tell her differently tomorrow.'

'But . . .' she tried to get in.

'How could I so disappoint her when you're convinced that she'll go absolutely dotty over my brother's child?'

Anstey swallowed on anger. 'I hate your logic,' she snapped, emotion getting to her at the picture of a sweet lady of mature years being devastated and bewildered when she took Rosie back to London with her tomorrow. 'I don't think, Mr Quartermaine,' she said mulishly, 'that we'd better ask your mother to have Rosie after all.'

'We won't have to.' He dumbfounded her once more. 'If my mother reacts the way you say she will to the child, then by tomorrow, she'll be insisting that Rosie stays behind. By the way,' he said, while she was taking that in, 'make it Cale.'

Stubbornly, Anstey refused to call him by his first name, or to say another word. The rest of the journey was completed in silence, with even the baby declining to make a sound.

Quiet Ways was a large country house, set in its own grounds. Anstey was riddled with last-minute misgivings when Cale halted the car on the drive in front of the impressive building. Holding Rosie tightly to her, she felt little reassurance when he touched her elbow and piloted her towards the wide and substantial front door. Urged through the door and across the thickly carpeted hall, Anstey thought that Cale seemed to know where his mother would be. He opened a door that led into a drawing-room.

Anstey's first sight of the aristocratic-looking lady who rose straight-backed from one of the chairs did nothing to quieten the apprehension she was feeling.

'Cale!' Mrs Quartermaine exclaimed, her eyes, blue like Lester's, flitting from her elder son to his female companion and the baby she held.

'I told you I'd be here today,' he answered, his tone, to Anstey's ears, teasing.

'I've been listening for your car, but I must have closed my eyes for a few minutes,' Mrs Quartermaine replied, unsmiling, and took a few steps to meet them in the centre of the room.

Anstey was just forming the view that by no chance was she going to leave Rosie with this frosty-looking woman, when several things happened all at the same time. Suddenly Rosie began to stir, and Mrs Quartermaine bent to have a close inspection of her. Knowing from past experience that Rosie would start yelling the moment she was awake, Anstey heard Cale say, 'Mother, this is Anastasia . . .' when, for the first time in her young life, on waking, Rosie looked up at her grandmother and beamed a most engaging smile, and then—gurgled happily!

Taken aback by the unknown phenomenon, Anstey saw that Cale too, who was better acquainted with the bad-tempered side of Rosie, appeared slightly amazed. Even his mother seemed to be put off her stride, Anstey noticed, for as Rosie beamed up at her, Mrs Quartermaine lost her frosty exterior, and actually smiled back!

'And who are you, you delightful child?' she asked the babe in cooing tones, quite forgetful that her son had not completed his other introduction.

'This,' said Cale, his eyes watchful on his parent as he obviously decided he could complete his introduction of Anstey when he had more of his mother's attention, 'is Rosie Tresilla Quartermaine.'

It was all he needed to say to have Mrs Quartermaine's undivided attention. 'Rosie—*Tresilla* . . .!' she gasped.

'The family name,' Cale nodded, and added quietly,

'Mother, this is your granddaughter.'

Astonishment kept Mrs Quartermaine silent for some seconds as, flabbergasted, she looked first to the baby, then to Anstey, and then to her son. 'Good gracious!' she managed to pull herself together to exclaim. 'When on earth did you get married?'

Straight away Anstey opened her mouth to disclaim any such idea. But, before she could even begin to say that not only was she not married to the elder son of the house, but also that the baby was not his offspring but Lester's, Cale was in first.

'I'm . . .' he said, and—remembering that Anstey was still there by his side—'We,' he amended, 'Anstey and I, are not married.'

'Not—married!' Wait for it, Anstey thought, realising as she watched Mrs Quartermaine's expression change that there was going to be trouble. She had thought her frosty before, but she now became poker-backed again as what her son had said sank in, and her face went tight with anger. 'How *dare* you?' she rounded on him. 'How dare you allow this child, *my* grandchild, to be brought into the world illegitimate?'

Grief! Clearly Cale's mother was mightily upset. Anstey looked to Cale and was mystified when he delayed explaining that it was his brother who was Rosie's father, and not him. Half inclined to do the explaining for him, Anstey hesitated. Plainly Mrs Quartermaine was outraged, so perhaps Cale, who knew her where she did not, was searching for the most tactful way to go about it.

The silence seemed to go on for ever. But when, tactful or not, Anstey knew she was going to have to say something, Rosie chose that moment to make her presence felt. Peeved that no one was paying her the slightest attention, she let go full throttle. With the tense atmosphere shattered by her persistent cries, it was left to Anstey to say apologetically, 'I don't think she'll stop until she's had her bottle.'

'You'd better show *Miss* ... up to the nursery,' Mrs Quartermaine addressed her son coldly.

'I thought we'd stay the night,' he suggested, to Anstey's amazement. Surely he could see that they weren't welcome—not now!

'It's your house,' Mrs Quartermaine replied stiffly. 'But while I'm under this roof, you and *your friend*,' she added, igniting Anstey to anger, 'will do me the courtesy of sleeping in separate rooms.'

Not trusting herself to speak, Anstey, with the howling baby in her arms, marched to the door. Had the baby not been howling for her feed, had not Cale come to take a firm hold on her arm and steer her towards the stairs, she was certain she would have followed her instinct and marched out of the front door and all the way back to London.

Neither of them said a word as they mounted the stairs, but, 'I'm not staying,' she told Cale sharply, once they were in a light and airy nursery.

'I'll go and get the gear in,' was his only answer as he abruptly departed.

He'll probably bring all the wrong things, Anstey fumed, anticipating that the 'gear' he had gone to collect was to be just enough for the baby's present needs.

Taking in her surroundings as she rocked and crooned to Rosie, she noticed that everywhere was spick and span. A mattressless cot stood in one corner, while another corner had been given over to washing and bottle-preparing facilities. Walking with Rosie was second nature, so Anstey walked over to where a communicating door stood open. She saw that the door led to a single bedroom, the sort of room a nanny might use to be within earshot of a new-born baby.

She moved back into the nursery as Cale returned laden with all she would need, and more. As if the sight of the bag with the lunch she was starved for was more than she could withstand, Rosie turned up the volume.

'Anything I can do?' Cale offered when Rosie paused for breath.

'No, thank you,' Anstey replied shortly. Cale left her to it.

An hour later, when he returned, she was seated in a nursing chair with Rosie sleepily sucking on the last of her feeding bottle.

'How's it going?' he asked, closing the door and pulling up another chair to come and sit down to survey the proceedings.

'Slowly,' Anstey replied.

'Feeling better?' he queried.

Several answers, most of them cutting, rose to her lips. 'I've never been made to feel like a—a tart, before,' she said flatly.

'My mother didn't mean . . .' He broke off. 'I'm sorry,' he apologised, and sounded so sincere that Anstey took her eyes from the baby to look at him. 'When I saw how taken she was with this vocal baggage,' he went on, his glance flicking to Rosie and back to Anstey, 'I'm afraid I gave not a thought to the construction she would put on my telling her that here was her granddaughter. Just,' he went on, his eyes holding Anstey's, 'as I never gave thought to how she would feel when she found that her granddaughter is illegitimate.'

Anstey saw that there was a warm look in his eyes suddenly, and, most peculiarly, all her anger melted and she felt compelled to tell him, 'If I'm honest, I never gave it a thought either.'

Ridiculously, her heart gave a most unexpected bump when Cale smiled a slow and gentle smile. Hastily she gave all her attention to the feeding infant. It took only a moment for her to realise that, since she was starting to feel a shade hungry herself, that bump in her heart region must be the result of some inverted kind of indigestion.

All the same, she kept her head bent when she reasoned, 'I expect it was something of a shock for your mother to suddenly learn she has a granddaughter. And I don't suppose,' she went on, 'that she's any more pleased with Lester than she was with you, now that you've told her that . . .'

'I—haven't told her.'

Anstey's head shot up. 'You haven't told her!' His smile had gone, she saw, but even then she was not particularly worried. 'You mean—you haven't had time to tell her that Lester is Rosie's father?' she asked, having thought the hour since she had seen him had been spent with him telling his mother the whole story.

'I mean,' Cale answered levelly, 'that I—can't tell her.'

'*Can't*!' she exclaimed, and didn't pause to wonder what it was about this man that made her normally even temperament so very short-lived. 'What do you mean, you *can't* tell her?' she challenged, already starting to get heated. 'Of course you can, you'll have to. You'll . . .'

'I said you were a little hothead,' he murmured, looking into her sparking eyes. 'Though, since I haven't been as totally open with you as I could have been,' he conceded, 'perhaps you have a right to be a—little angry.'

Anstey's senses pounced on his admission that he had not been as open with her as he could have been, and suddenly she was wary. She had known in advance that he was a hard man, a man who could end his own brother's career without a thought. But all at once she had the dreadful feeling that his talk at her flat of not being able to turn his back on his flesh and blood might have been just so much eye-wash. Had he in fact, all along, been just using her and Rosie for some diabolical purpose of his own? Anstey thought it was more than high time that she found out.

'Perhaps, Mr Quartermaine,' she addressed him coldly, feeling such enmity against him then that she would cut her tongue out rather than use his first name, 'you could bring yourself to tell me the truth about why you've brought Rosie and me here.' He didn't like her tone, she knew that when his eyes narrowed and forewarned her that he was just as likely to tell her she could take a running jump before he would account to her for anything. 'It wasn't for Rosie's benefit, or mine either, was it?' she challenged sharply.

'Not—entirely,' he conceded, after some moments of deliberation. 'Though the child is of some concern to me, which is why I called to see you last Tuesday.' Anstey reckoned she could be grateful that his concern was only for Rosie, and not her. Friends like him she could do without.

'You wanted to see what sort of a hovel she was being brought up in, no doubt,' she offered acidly.

'That,' he agreed sternly, 'and to talk about financial matters.'

'There's more to it than that!' Anstey snapped. Having had the wool pulled over her eyes once, she was not ready to let it happen a second time. 'You'd already got some Machiavellian plan worked out before you so much as knocked at my door,' she accused.

'Machiavellian?' he echoed in some surprise. 'I assure you the only plan I had was to ensure . . .'

'That Rosie and I came here with you today,' Anstey cut him off hotly.

'That idea was never in my head,' he said, and added succinctly, 'until you put it there.'

'I put it there?' she scoffed.

Cale Quartermaine nodded. 'You were so certain that grandmothers go gaga at their first grandchild that you had me convinced, too. You said,' he reminded her as if every unthinking word she had said on the subject was indelibly printed on his brain, 'that—were Rosie yours—

once your mother had got over the shock, she would be ready to forgive you anything. I couldn't help wondering,' he ended, 'if my mother, too, would forgive her offspring anything, once she had become acquainted with his child.'

Momentarily, Anstey was perplexed. 'Your mother has something to forgive you for?'

'Not me,' he said quietly.

'Lester?' she queried, and wanted to know, 'What's he done?'

'What hasn't he done?' Cale asked, and seemed reluctant to blacken his brother's name, until suddenly, he said, 'Hell, the fact that he's acted as such a bastard to your friend shows you know he's no angel. That,' he said distastefully, 'is what comes from overindulging a child.'

'Lester was overindulged?' she questioned, forgetting for a moment that she intended to keep her wits about her lest Cale lead her further up the garden path. Quickly she brought herself up short. 'I thought it was you who was the spoiled one,' she said forthrightly. 'According to what Lester told Joanna, you were the favourite who could do no wrong.'

'According to Lester,' said Cale with equal forthright-ness, 'everyone's out of step but him. The fact is that, as a long-awaited second child, my brother was much wanted, much loved—and spoiled beyond all reason. He grew into a man who, although he has many redeeming qualities, has some traits which are far from likeable.'

'Breaking my friend's heart, for one,' Anstey put in sourly.

'Your friend is not the only female who's experienced heartbreak over him,' Cale told her shortly.

'He makes a habit of making women believe he's desperately in love with them and . . .!'

'No,' Cale cut in, 'not as far as I know. I was speaking of

the heartbreak he has caused, and is still causing his mother.'

'Mrs Quartermaine . . .' Anstey didn't finish. Everybody had an outer self they showed the world, she supposed, but somehow she couldn't equate that frosty-faced woman with heartbreak. On reflection, though, it could well be that her frosty manner stemmed *from* that heartbreak.

Suddenly Anstey realised that she was softening. She was making firmer efforts to be as hard as Cale, when he continued, 'His mother idolised him. Take that as fact, as truth, and you'll see that when he decided, a year or so ago, to start his own business . . .'

'After you had so heartlessly, without love or notice, dismissed him,' Anstey inserted in her toughening-up attempt.

Cale hesitated, then merely said, 'You know more than I thought. But yes, after I threw him out on his ear, he had this grand scheme that was going to make his millions. Unfortunately,' he went on, 'his scheme needed to have thousands invested before it could get off the ground. Thousands which he hadn't got.'

Anstey caught on fast. 'Your mother—she lent him the money?'

'Unbeknown to me,' nodded Cale. 'To the extent of mortgaging this house.'

The picture he was drawing started to become clearer. 'The firm he started went bust—and your mother was heartbroken when he couldn't pay her back?' Anstey suggested.

'It wasn't losing the money so much that hurt her, but Lester's careless attitude when, at the end of her rope and having visions of being turned out of her beloved home, he appeared not to care a damn. There followed one God-awful quarrel where the fur really flew. It ended up with his mother telling him that she would never forgive him, and never wanted to see him again. Lester's parting words were that he'd see her dead first.'

'My heavens!' Anstey exclaimed, her voice hushed. As Cale had said, it must have been an awful quarrel.

'My heavens,' Cale returned crisply, 'is polite compared to what I said when I eventually got to hear of it.'

'Your mother didn't tell you straight away?'

'I doubt I'd know now,' he replied, 'but for a chance happening. I knew something was wrong, but couldn't get from her what it was. She loves this house, so it just didn't tie up when she began talking in terms of the house being too big for her.'

'She was getting ready to move out?'

Again he nodded. 'She would have done, too, had I not chanced to use her bank when on one of my visits I ran short of ready cash.' His expression was grim when he revealed, 'I thought to change a cheque would only take a minute, but once inside, I was buttonholed by the bank manager who wanted to give me his personal apology, and explain that he'd had no option but to foreclose on Quiet Ways.'

'It—must have been something of a shock,' Anstey said, and quickly realised that he must have taken immediate steps to prevent the foreclosure, when she remembered, 'Your mother—she said this is your house.'

'Purely as a precaution against the same thing happening again, I had the property made over to my name. But,' he muttered, 'it's her house, and she knows it is. Not,' he added, 'that I need have worried—Lester hasn't been near since the day they had a stand-up row, and said such bitterly wounding things to each other.' He fixed Anstey with a straight look and said quietly, 'Which brings me to the main reason why you and the infant are here; the reason why I cannot—for the moment—tell my mother that Rosie's father is Lester. And,' he said, 'the reason why I should like your—co-operation.'

'I'm listening,' Anstey invited warily.

'To begin with,' Cale took her up on her wary invite, 'it causes my mother great pain and distress that it's now nearly a year since she last saw my brother. I've seen her grow more and more—vinegary—with each passing month, and all because, although she's too proud to admit it, she's hurting like hell inside.'

Anstey started to feel a chink in her armour. She didn't like the feeling. 'What about Lester?' she asked, in an endeavour to take the conversation away from the woman whose only reward for idolising her younger son had been pain.

'Lester,' Cale said heavily, 'is being at his stubborn worst.'

'You've seen him?'

'Some time ago,' Cale admitted, and shrugged. 'I suppose it wasn't conducive to healing the breach that I felt more like punching the life out of him for what he'd done than asking him to go to Quiet Ways to give his mother some peace of mind.'

'He refused?'

'He dug his heels in, and said Mother knew where *he* lived if she wanted to apologise for all she'd said.'

Anstey decided she didn't want to discuss Lester, or his stubbornness either. The whole of Joanna's problems had started when he had been particularly mulish when she wouldn't have an abortion.

'They'll both come round in time, I expect,' she said, trying to sound hard.

'Time,' Cale countered, 'is going on, and my mother, beside not getting any younger, is not happy. Financially,' he went on, 'I can give her everything she wants; but money can't buy that which she wants most—a reconciliation with my brother.'

'But you said—that she'd vowed never to forgive him!'

'And you said,' Cale tossed back, 'that a mother would forgive anything on being presented with her first grandchild.'

'Ah!' Suddenly it was all clear. 'So *that's* why Rosie and I are here!'

'I admit it,' he replied, without so much as a blink at his deviousness. 'But my plan went badly wrong when my mother all but had apoplexy on realising that her grandchild is illegitimate.'

'Which is why,' Anstey quickly worked it out, taking a glance at the baby to see that she had fallen asleep over her bottle, 'you feel you can't tell her that Rosie is Lester's child. Because . . .'

'Because,' Cale took up, 'from her moral viewpoint, she'd deem it a more unforgivable sin than anything he's ever done before. Don't you see,' he asked, 'that should I tell her the truth, far from ending the rift as I intended, that rift will be made wider than ever?'

Anstey did see. Never would she forget Mrs Quartermaine's expression when Cale had told her that she and he were not married. Never would she forget Mrs Quartermaine's outrage when she had rounded on Cale and asked him 'How dare you allow this child, *my* grandchild, to be brought into the world illegitimate?' Anstey saw for herself that any hope Cale had of a reconciliation between his mother and Lester would be gone if she learned the true facts.

'But . . .' she said, feeling as if she was fighting without ammunition, 'we—you can't allow her to go on believing that Rosie is yours!'

The steely look that came to Cale's eyes warned her that she was going to be on the receiving end of a blunt 'Why can't I?' It did not come. Seconds passed, during which he studied her set expression which said she would oppose him all the way on this issue.

Then, 'What harm will it do?' he asked solemnly. 'It's not as if we're trying to foist someone else's grandchild on to her, is it? Rosie *is* her flesh-and-blood granddaughter, after all.'

'Yes, but . . .'

'She's already greatly hurt,' He cut her off. 'Do you wish to cause her more pain?' He applied none-too-gentle pressure on her sensitivities. 'Can you not, Anstey,' he kept up that pressure, 'go along with me until I find the right moment, the moment when I feel she'll be able to hear the truth?'

Anstey's soft heart was touched, and she had no wish for anyone to feel more pain. But it just wasn't *right*! She had to make a stand. Cale Quartermaine was making a habit of jet-propelling her along—it was time to call a halt.

'No,' she said firmly. 'It's not on! To go along with you,' she said quickly when it looked as though he was going to interrupt, 'would cause your mother to assume, naturally, that I am Rosie's mother. That——' She would have charged on, only she was interrupted just the same.

'That—surely—can only be to the good,' he cut in.

'I'm—not with you,' Anstey said slowly, and felt a sudden premonition of disaster when Cale leaned back in his chair, and looked so casual it wasn't true—to let fall softly, 'As Rosie's mother, my dear Anstey, no one can prevent you from taking her back to London tomorrow—if that's what you wish.'

Darts of alarm started to spear her. 'Just—what—are you saying?' she asked while trying to hold down panic.

'Work it out for yourself,' he offered, but did the job for her when all she was capable of was to stare at him. 'Surely you can see that we, as blood relatives, can take all rights from you?'

'You—can't!' she gasped. 'You wouldn't!' she amended

as it hit her sharply that that—he could!

He shrugged. 'I can't guarantee my mother wouldn't,' he said, and actually smiled, a smile she didn't like at all, when he added, 'But it won't come to that—if you play things my way.'

Anstey was aware then that Cale Quartermaine had nursed that final ace up his sleeve the whole time in case she proved difficult—and she hated him for it. There seemed no end to his quick thinking, to his deviousness. She, as a non-blood-relative assigned only verbally as guardian, hadn't a legal leg to stand on. Only now did she recognise that fact, but Cale Quartermaine—he had recognised and known it from the beginning!

'Well?' he asked, as though thinking he had given her all the time she needed.

Damn him, Anstey thought, he knew full well that she could do nothing but agree! 'What do grown-ups do for lunch around here?' she snapped, determined not to give him vocal consent.

She knew he was aware that he had won when he eased his long length from his chair. 'If you can leave the infant,' he said pleasantly, casting an eye at the sleeping Rosie, 'I'll take you to the ...'

'I'm not leaving her,' Anstey cut him off tartly.

'Then I'll have a tray sent up,' he answered mildly, and left her—to hate him some more. He didn't care whom he used! Granite was softer than him!

CHAPTER FOUR

TRUE to his word, Cale had a lunch tray sent up. Anstey was still reeling from the trap she considered she had walked into when a well-rounded lady somewhere in her middle fifties came in with her lunch.

'Aren't you gorgeous?' the woman crooned, no sooner placing down her tray then she was bending over the sleeping Rosie. 'I'm sorry,' she quickly whispered in apology when she spared a moment to look at Anstey. 'I'm Netty Lewis. I've been just itching to come and have a look at the baby ever since Mrs Quartermaine told me she was here, and asked if I'd like to put in a few more hours.'

'I'm Anstey Eldridge,' Anstey introduced herself, and murmured an apology of her own when she added, 'I expect an extra couple of people in the house does make for extra work.'

'Oh, there's plenty of staff to cope,' Netty Lewis answered warmly. 'I've been asked to help with this sweet love.' And before Anstey had time to make any comment, 'You don't mind, do you?' she asked. 'Only I jumped at the chance. I used to look after Mrs Quartermaine's two, and I've had four children of my own,' she went on rapidly, as if thinking she was about to be asked for references.

Anstey observed the anxiety in the woman's eyes and, more to try to put her at her ease than anything else, asked, 'You live locally, Mrs Lewis?'

'In the village, and please call me Netty,' she replied. 'So it's all right,' she asked anxiously, 'if I help you with the baby?'

Anstey was torn, but in view of the woman's anxious expression, she told her, 'If you'd like to.'

'Would I ever!' Netty replied enthusiastically. 'Shall I hold her while you eat your lunch?'

Strictly speaking, Rosie could have slept just as soundly in the carry-cot which Cale had brought up. But Anstey could not miss the eagerness on the other woman's face.

'Of course,' she said.

'It's like old times,' said Netty, content as she took the baby from Anstey. That Netty Lewis loved children was plain for anyone to see.

The talk, as Anstey ate her meal and Netty settled herself in a nursing chair, was all about babies. Netty Lewis, Anstey learned, was a walking encyclopedia when it came to infant fads and fancies, having reared four of her own, each with different likes and dislikes. She had just finished saying how she had coped when her youngest had gone through a phase of not wanting to eat, when she volunteered suddenly, 'I expect you've some washing with you for this little sweetheart; I'll do that, then I'll make up the bed in there.' She pointed to the small adjoining bedroom. 'Mrs Quartermaine asked me if I could sleep in tonight,' she went on to explain, 'so I'll be nice and handy if Rosie . . .'

'I thought,' Anstey butted in, too startled to realise quite when she had revised her statement that she was not staying, 'that I'd use that room tonight.'

'Oh!' Netty exclaimed. 'But Mrs Collins has prepared a room for you down the landing. I know she has because I saw Cale take a weekend case in there ages ago.'

'Oh!' it was Anstey's turn to exclaim. She had the very definite feeling that events were going out of her control when, as though thinking that she did not trust her, Netty promptly stated,

'I won't let you down, Miss Eldridge, I promise. I'm so used to children, having had four of my own,' she reiterated, 'that I got into the habit years ago of sleeping with one ear always on the listen.'

'I'm sure you won't let me down,' Anstey told her sincerely, 'but . . .'

'If you're worried that I might neglect my own family, you've no cause,' Netty said quickly. 'All my youngsters have left home now, and . . .' she faltered, and an expression of sadness came to her face '. . . and since Bill, my husband, died last year, there's been nothing to rush home for.'

All of a sudden, Anstey's heartstrings were pulled. With four children, a husband and a home to look after, Netty Lewis must have had a full and busy life. Yet now, her children having left home, her husband gone, she must not only feel redundant and bereft, but also exceedingly lonely. Her statement, 'There's nothing to rush home for', endorsed that.

'My only worry,' said Anstey, finding she just didn't have what it took to harden her heart, 'is that Rosie can be a bit of a handful. She cries a lot—particularly at night,' she warned. 'You won't get much sleep, I'm afraid.'

'I know all about that.' Netty was suddenly all smiles. 'Our Jack was a demon! I wore many a floorboard out walking up and down with him in the early hours of the morning.'

Anstey's confidence in Netty Lewis grew when shortly afterwards Rosie awoke and cried unceasingly. Instinctively she would have taken over but, holding back, she was able to observe how calm, capable and completely unflustered the woman was as she crooned and soothed tirelessly.

Eventually Rosie's exertions made her sleepy again. 'It won't hurt her to have a walk along the landing,' Netty proclaimed. 'Would you like me to show you your room?'

The room Netty took her to was smart and elegant. 'It's a beautiful room,' Anstey told her, as she spotted her weekend case down by the end of the bed. Sensing that Netty couldn't wait to have the baby all to herself, she asked, 'Can you manage Rosie while I unpack?'

Netty's reply was to make a bee-line for the door. 'I'm sure I can,' she said happily.

Anstey held back from returning straight to the nursery when her small unpacking was done. Netty, she had soon realised, was in her element. When the time drew near for Rosie's six o'clock feed, though, she left her room.

The nursery was at the far end of the landing, but as she was nearing it, the door opened and Mrs Quartermaine came out. There had been a smile on the older woman's face. It abruptly vanished when she saw Anstey.

'Your room is satisfactory, Miss Eldridge?' she enquired, inner breeding demanding that even a frowned-upon guest should not go without a hostess's basic courtesy.

'Perfectly, thank you,' Anstey replied in kind.

'Then I shall see you at dinner at seven-thirty.' The aristocratic lady inclined her head, and sailed past.

Oh dear, Anstey thought, and reckoned that Cale Quartermaine was going to have a mighty long wait if he was still intent on not telling his mother the truth about Rosie until she was in a more receptive frame of mind. From what she had just seen, that stiff and starchy lady would still be believing that she and Cale were Rosie's parents when they left tomorrow.

That thought brought a reminder of his 'That—surely—can only be to the good.' His, 'As Rosie's mother, my dear Anstey, no one can prevent you from taking her back to London tomorrow.'

Darts of panic started to spear again as she realised the vulnerability of her position. Quickly, as if to outstrip nightmarish thoughts, she turned the handle of the nursery door. Rosie would soon be demanding her tea.

'Everything all right?' she asked Netty, but she could see for herself, as Netty turned away from a small hot-plate, that everything was going swimmingly.

'We've had a lovely afternoon,' she beamed. 'I'm just getting Rosie's bottle. She's just had a top-and-tail wash, and now,' she said, looking to where the infant had been temporarily placed in her carry-cot, 'we're going to have our tea, aren't we, my lovely?' she addressed the baby.

'She's been—good?' Anstey enquired, restraining an instinctive urge to take over.

'So-so,' Netty replied. 'She was on her best behaviour when Mrs Collins came up to make friends with her. But she didn't care too much for Mr Collins when he came up with the mattress for the cot.'

'Mattress!' Ansty slewed round to see that where before there had been no mattress in the cot, now there was one.

'It's all right,' Netty assured her quickly, 'it's been well aired. Mrs Quartermaine sent Cale out to buy it as soon as you got here. She personally supervised that every heater in the house was used on it when he brought it back. She checked it again when she came up just now.' Rosie's bottle ready, and tested for the correct temperature, Netty took her from her carry-cot. 'Your grandmother's no end taken with you, isn't she, my precious?' she crooned as she sat down with her.

Anstey took the chair which Cale had used earlier, and watched the never-forgotten expertise with which Netty handled the baby.

'I saw Mrs Quartermaine as she left just now,' Anstey said, not too certain how she felt about the statement that Rosie's grandmother was 'no end taken' with her grand-daughter. 'She seemed—er—happy from her visit.' Happy was perhaps overstating it, Anstey thought, but there had definitely been a smile on Mrs Quartermaine's face—until she had noticed her coming along the landing.

'She was just like she used to be before Lester ...' Hurriedly, as if suddenly aware that she might be speaking out of turn, Netty broke off and, bending her head to Rosie, she mumbled, 'But I dare say you know all about the way he's forgotten he ever had a mother.' Still quiet so as not to startle Rosie, her voice was clearer when she said, 'But who wouldn't be happy to be a grandmother—especially to this little darling.'

Anstey thought it time to take the conversation away from the subject of the Quartermaines. 'You don't have any grandchildren yet, Netty?'

'I keep hoping,' she answered. 'I've got two married daughters, and they're both good girls to their mum. But they're both more interested in having the latest microwave and dishwasher than in making me the happiest woman in the world.'

Anstey stayed in the nursery chatting to Netty while she fed and attended to the baby. When seven o'clock came, she would by far have preferred to have eaten her dinner in the nursery. But with Netty more able to cope with Rosie than she was herself, by the look of it, and with Mrs Quartermaine, albeit reluctantly, observing the manners of a hostess, Anstey realised that she too, as a guest, owed Mrs Quartermaine certain courtesies in return.

'I must dash,' she told Netty, 'or I'm going to be late for dinner.'

Back in her room, she went to the adjoining bathroom, had a quick wash and applied a light film of moisturiser to her face. Clad in her bra and briefs, she went to survey the two cotton dresses she had hung in the wardrobe. Past experience of caring for Rosie had proved it the height of folly to don anything that couldn't easily be washed. Hoping that she wasn't in a household that dressed for dinner, Anstey had just elected to wear the straw-pink cotton when there was a tap on the door. Her watch showed it was twenty minutes past seven.

Thinking to save time, she opted to hold her dress in front of her rather than to put the dress down and get into her robe. Without so much as a dab of powder on her nose, she went and opened the door a crack.

'Yes?' she enquired sharply of the lounge-suited Cale Quartermaine, not taken with the way his right eyebrow raised itself a fraction, or the quirk of amusement she was sure was pulling at the corners of his mouth.

'Charming,' he drawled, but whether at her snappy 'Yes' or at the shiny-faced picture she represented, she didn't know. 'Not ready yet, I see,' he murmured, resting his eyes on her bare, apart from bra strap, shoulder. 'Dinner's at seven-thirty,' he added, amusement definitely there as she pulled her shoulder back from his view. 'Er—shall I wait?' he asked, and gave her the benefit of his white even teeth.

'I'll find my own way down!' Anstey snapped, and shut the door in his face.

A second later, her own white, even teeth were in evidence. Why she should think the exchange had been funny, though, was beyond her. Abruptly, she cancelled her smile. Strangely, however, the grin she had witnessed on Cale's face—for positively, he had grinned at her—was harder to banish from her mind.

Seven minutes later she galloped from her room, to slow down to a more sedate pace as she turned to descend the wide and gracious staircase.

'One minute to go,' said Cale, appearing from nowhere as she reached the bottom of the stairs. So saying, he took a grip of her elbow and escorted her along the hall to the dining-room.

She took a deep breath and felt no little disquiet as he opened the door and stood back for her to precede him. Everything in her was against lying to his mother, but since she couldn't see the whole of the meal being got through without the subject of Rosie coming up, Anstey anticipated a very uncomfortable time.

Her surmise that it would be just the three of them at dinner appeared to be inaccurate, however. A tubby man, his clerical collar denoting that he was a man of the cloth, stood over by the fireplace in conversation with her hostess as Cale, his hand still at her elbow, urged her forwards.

It was apparent that Cale and the minister had met

before, for it was Cale who performed the introductions.
Some of Anstey's apprehension departed. Quite obviously
the Reverend Mr Midwinter had been invited to dine at
Quiet Ways before Mrs Quartermaine had known Cale
would be paying a visit this weekend. From what she had so
far seen of Mrs Quartermaine, it therefore followed that it
would be against her strict ethics to cancel some
longstanding arrangement merely because her son had
brought an unexpected guest with him. But at all events,
Anstey reckoned she could be pretty sure that no mention
would be made in front of the vicar of her other unexpected
guest—the illegitimate babe.

Breathing more easily, Anstey took the chair which Cale
held out for her at the dining-table. It was an oval table,
and she watched as he strode round to the other side and
took the chair across from her.

A small, thin woman whom Anstey guessed was Mrs
Collins promptly arrived to serve the first course, and no
sooner had she gone than Mrs Quartermaine started the
conversational ball rolling.

'Anastasia's family live in Suffolk,' she informed the
vicar. 'I believe you once had a parish in that area.'

'Indeed I did,' he replied, and while Anstey quickly
realised that Mrs Quartermaine must have given Cale a
thorough grilling about her, for that information could
have come from no one but him, the vicar was asking,
'What part of Suffolk do you hail from, Miss Eldridge?'

Keeping her wits about her, Anstey told him, but
although he had heard of Long Kinnington, he knew no
one from her village. Anstey grew more confident, and
with the possibility eliminated of talk getting back to Long
Kinnington about her or, should Rosie be mentioned, the
baby, she chatted comfortably with him on the beauty of
Suffolk, until the next course was served.

Of the belief that it wasn't courteous to hog all of the
meal-time conversation, Anstey remained silent when the

vicar began to regale them with matters pertaining to his
present parish. She listened attentively just the same, but
when Cale made some comment and she looked at his
serious expression, she was somehow diverted to remember
how he had stood, not serious but with a grin on his face, at
the door of her room.

It seemed impossible then that such a serious man should
own such a grin! Anstey came to an awarness that
conversation was still going on around her when, suddenly,
she realised that she was staring at Cale's mouth just as if she
was willing him to show her his grin again!

Good heavens, she thought, and gave herself a mental
shake. Swiftly she took her eyes from him, and gave all her
energies to trying to pick up the threads of the conversation
now going on between the minister and Mrs Quartermaine. Apparently, she tuned in, there was to be a wedding
in the village shortly.

'In the circumstances,' Mrs Quartermaine was saying,
casting a glance to Cale and back to the vicar, 'it will be a
quiet wedding.'

Anstey did not follow Mrs Quartermaine's glance to
Cale. She had no wish to again become side-tracked,
although certainly she had no interest in finding out if that
grin she had seen had been his one and only. She kept her
eyes on Mrs Quartermaine, guessing, as the subject of the
quiet wedding continued, that the reason it was to be a
quiet one must be because someone from either the bride's
family or the groom's family had suffered a recent
bereavement. But, quiet or no, it appeared that Mrs
Quartermaine would be attending, and that she expected
Cale would attend also.

A minute later, with shock, and not a little horror,
Anstey was made to realise that so too would *she* be
expected to attend this wedding. That, in fact, it was *her*
wedding they were discussing!

'I can rely on you, Anastasia, I hope,' Mrs Quartermaine

fixed her with a straight look, 'not to wear white.'

'I'm—sorry?' Anstey queried, in something of a fog, but even so feeling prickles of apprehension ripple up her spine.

'The village gossips will have enough to wag their tongues over when they hear that my granddaughter was born out of wedlock,' Mrs Quartermaine answered stiffly, 'without your giving them further cause to ridicule the name of Quartermaine by arriving to be married dressed in that pure shade.'

There was much in Mrs Quartermaine's reply to which Anstey could have taken exception. But, shaken to the core to realise that she had sat there like a dummy and let all this talk of her wedding go on, all she could do was to stare in utter astonishment.

Grappling with shock and horror, Anstey realised that not only did the vicar know all about Rosie, but that there had been nothing longstanding about his invitation to dine that night at Quiet Ways! Clearly, Mrs Quartermaine could not tolerate the fact that her granddaughter was illegitimate, and had taken immediate steps to do something about it!

Stunned, Anstey switched her astonished gaze from Mrs Quartermaine to find that Cale had been sitting silently watching her. He had registered that she was absolutely dumbfounded, of that Anstey was sure, but although he met her look of horror steadily, his expression was bland.

Unable to see why he was keeping quiet, why he wasn't saying something—anything—suddenly, Anstey was on her guard. She had no clue to what was going on in his sharp brain, but she had come up against his deviousness before. It could be, of course, that he was not denying that they were to be married simply so as not to embarrass his mother in front of the vicar. But—and much more likely—should he have some other devious scheme already worked out, Anstey decided right then that she was not going to be a party to it.

'Actually, Mrs Quartermaine,' she turned back to her hostess when it was all too obvious that she was going to get no help from Cale, 'there will be no wedding.' Mrs Quartermaine's expression did not become merely frosty, it appeared carved from ice when, making certain there should be no mistake, Anstey went on to state, 'Cale and I are not going to be married.'

A deathly silence followed, and given that the dining-room carpet was as lush and as thick as the carpets in the rest of the house, Anstey was sure she would have heard it had a pin dropped. But having, so to speak, set the cat among the pigeons, it was not she who received the sharp edge of Mrs Quartermaine's tongue. Her stiff composure quickly recovered, Mrs Quartermaine fastened her highly displeased glance on Cale, and witheringly reminded him, 'Your dear dead father instilled in you a sense of honour. Your conduct thus far has not only dishonoured your father's name, but his memory also. So tell me plainly,' she went on coldly, 'have you any intention to now act more honourably towards this young woman? Do you, as your father's son, intend to marry her?'

A hush again descended on the room, during which Anstey even felt a fleeting sympathy with Lester if, in his quarrel with his mother, she had attacked him in the same forthright way. But it was Cale who was in the hot seat now, and, bearing in mind that he had left it to her to tell his mother that there was not going to be any wedding, Anstey couldn't see why he shouldn't take some of the flak. She might even find a trace of enjoyment in watching the confirmed bachelor wriggle.

She spared him a look. He spared her a smile. That smile was still on his face when he replied smoothly, 'I rather think, Mother of mine, that Anstey would not marry me even should I be so bold as to ask her.'

'Surely you're not afraid to ask her?' Mrs Quartermaine, looking and sounding amazed, took him literally.

'I'd just die if he did,' Anstey put in, suddenly finding that she had a decided aversion to Mrs Quartermaine thinking she would leap at the chance to marry her odious elder son. 'And Cale,' she added, in no doubt about how much he valued his bachelorhood, 'would be promptly wheeled off to the intensive care ward of some cardiac unit, should I be bold enough to say yes.'

'Perhaps,' interceded Mr Midwinter, when Mrs Quartermaine looked momentarily perplexed by this modern way of going on, 'we'd better leave the—er—umph—happy couple to—hmp—discuss the matter—a little further.'

'There's nothing to discuss.' Anstey turned to the vicar to smile. And in case Mrs Quartermaine wasn't convinced and still imagined that she was waiting with bated breath for Cale to pop the question, she stretched the truth about her run-of-the-mill job at Elton Diesel. 'I have my career . . .'

'You're working!' Mrs Quartermaine butted in to exclaim before she could say more.

'Not . . . I'm having some time off,' Anstey recovered and found another smile. 'I have my career,' she restated. 'I just don't need the encumbrance of a husband.'

'You should have thought of your career,' Mrs Quartermaine said waspishly, to send her smile flying, 'before you encumbered yourself with a baby!'

To find that she too had been rounded on, and in front of company, stung. And in the heat of an angry moment, Anstey forgot entirely why it was that Cale did not want his mother to know the truth of Rosie's parentage. In her view she'd taken enough from this strong-minded woman with her black and white vision that allowed no shade of grey. It was about time a little truth was aired around here.

Unaware of Cale's eyes sharp on her, Anstey began 'Rosie . . .' but was promptly chopped off.

'Rosie,' Cale cut in sharply, causing her to look at him

and to observe the no-nonsense look in his eyes, 'is no encumbrance. Nor,' he said sternly, 'will she be. If Anstey will not marry me,' he stated, for all the world as though she had turned him down, 'then she will not. But either way,' he continued, pinning Anstey's eyes with his own, 'the responsibility for the infant—is mine.'

Cold fear clutched at Anstey's heart. She opened her mouth to protest, but nothing came out. She remembered his 'Surely you can see that we, as blood relatives, can take all rights from you', and she knew then, without a shadow of a doubt, that one wrong word from her and the decision of whether she took Rosie back to London with her tomorrow or not would be taken from her. Cale Quartermaine had the upper hand.

'Your *chivalry*,' Mrs Quartermaine opined acidly, when she and everyone else at the table knew that, for the moment, the subject was closed, 'does you credit.'

Anstey was never more glad than when the meal came to an end. Cale had tried to engage both her and his mother in other conversation, but neither of them viewed him as their favourite person just then. Not that it bothered him. He thereafter ignored them, and invited the vicar to give forth—which he did at length—on the merits of the village cricket team.

'If you'll excuse me,' Anstey said, when Mrs Quartermaine had suggested that they adjourn to the drawing-room to take coffee, 'I'll go and look in on Rosie.'

'Of course,' Mrs Quartermaine concurred, and for once almost smiled at her as if she was every bit in favour of Anstey's show of maternalism.

Anstey could have done without Cale leaving his chair to escort her to the dining-room door. As, too, she could have done without his salute to her cheek when, because his mother had decreed that they had separate rooms, he saw it as his duty not to let her go without a goodnight kiss. Her heart gave an erratic jump when his lips touched her skin, and his breath was warm upon her when he murmured, 'I'll see you in the morning, darling.'

'Unfortunately,' she muttered so that only he could hear, and when he gave a short laugh she was sufficiently confused that, notwithstanding that her heart gave another erratic jump, she could not tell if his laugh was genuine or if it was an act because his mother was watching.

But for decorum, Anstey would have taken the stairs three at a time the quicker to get away from him. She hurried just the same but, strangely, where Cale's kiss had made her heart thump, her hurried ascent of the stairs had no such effect.

It was her firm opinion then, what with everything else in her life gone crazy, that the fact that her heart should behave out of sequence with events was no more than was to be expected. She entered the nursery, and cast Cale Quartermaine to the devil.

CHAPTER FIVE

IT was half past one in the morning when Anstey's recently built-in alarm system brought her awake. A minute later she had donned her robe, and was silently pattering along to the nursery.

Still shaking cobwebs of sleep away, she went in to see that Netty Lewis, with a wide-awake Rosie in her arms, was already engaged in preparing the two o'clock feed.

'I'll take over if you like, Netty,' Anstey volunteered, going over to give Rosie a smile. 'I expect you're worn out from walking the floor with this cherub,' she added a shade guiltily, having not heard so much as a peep, but guessing that Rosie had been exercising her lungs.

'She's been a bit fretful, but nothing I haven't dealt with before,' Netty replied, and without self-pity, she confided, 'I don't sleep well since Bill died, so I'm glad to have something to do during those worst hours. Rosie will be all right if you want to go back to bed,' she went on, and added cheerily, 'And you can trust me to see that she gets her six o'clock bottle too.'

'I'm sure I can,' Anstey smiled and, taking the hint, she went back to bed.

She came to the surface again at half past five, looked at her watch with one eye open, and remembered Netty's 'You can trust me . . .' Anstey hesitated for a few moments, then snuggled down and went back to sleep.

The next time she awakened, the sun was streaming through her window. Sunday had dawned as bright as the previous day. After a bad start, summer had arrived, and the weather was settled.

Anstey got out of bed, and was anything but settled. She was just thinking that she would have a quick bath and then go along to the nursery to see how Netty was coping with Rosie when her thoughts flitted past Rosie, and on to Cale Quartermaine.

The cold hand of fear again grabbed at her when she remembered how, at dinner last night, he had claimed responsibility for Rosie, and Anstey started to hate him afresh. He had not been joking, she knew that for a certainty. But, if she was to keep Rosie safe for Joanna, then for a certainty too, she was going to have to play the game his way.

Disliking what she had so innocently walked into, Anstey did not like herself very much either. Desperation had driven her to his office in the first place. He, callous swine that he was, hadn't taken long to make the fullest capital of the situation, though, had he? She recalled his visit to the flat, and she hated him some more because, within seconds of her telling him the one thing that would have a grandmother ready to forgive her offspring anything, his devious mind had it all planned, all worked out.

Anstey's thinking became a trifle clouded when a small, honest voice pointed out to her that none of Cale's actions had been for his own benefit. His endeavours, as devious as they were, were all aimed at ending his mother's hurt and getting her to forgive Lester so that they could be reconciled.

Anstey batted away any extenuating circumstances her innate honesty had pushed to the fore. He was a devious swine, and hard with it, and that was all there was to it. She was then bombarded by a memory of his kiss to her cheek, and of his genuine-sounding short laugh when her reply of 'Unfortunately' had seemed to amuse him. She still wasn't sure if that bark of laughter had been genuine, but she discovered suddenly that the memory of his kiss, and of his laughter, had made her thinking more clouded than ever. Because, when it came to the other part of his devious plan, the part which would enable her to be at her desk tomorrow, she just did not know if she wanted it to work or not.

Her first sight of Mrs Quartermaine yesterday had made her certain that no way was she going to leave Rosie at Quiet Ways. Since then though, it had become apparent that while Mrs Quartermaine had no time for one Anstey Eldridge, the older woman would protect her granddaughter with nothing short of her life. Added to that was the fact that Netty Lewis was a gem and could be trusted to take the greatest care of Rosie. And, if she left all that aside and got down to practicalities, Anstey realised that if she didn't put in an appearance at Elton Diesel tomorrow, she could well find herself out of a job—a job which was vital to her.

More muddled than ever, she went and had her bath. She had donned a fresh cotton dress and was on her way to see Rosie when she realised that there was nothing she could do but to wait and see. She might not even have that decision to make about leaving her. Cale had said his mother would insist that Rosie stayed behind at Quiet Ways, but so far Anstey had seen no sign of Mrs Quartermaine insisting on anything other than that she and Cale should get married.

Netty was in the middle of bathing Rosie when Anstey went in. 'She's a tidy size for her age, isn't she?' Netty offered, looking up.

'You don't think she's overweight?' Anstey asked quickly.

'Not a bit of it,' Netty replied stoutly. 'She's just sturdy—she takes after the Yoxhalls.'

'Mrs Quartermaine was a Yoxhall, wasn't she,' said

Anstey conversationally as she sat down.

'That she was,' Netty agreed, and added, 'I didn't get to give this young lady her six o'clock bottle, after all.'

'She hasn't been fed!' exclaimed Anstey in alarm, though she realised almost at once that that couldn't be so or by now Rosie would be screaming the place down.

'Mrs Quartermaine came in and, sitting where you are now, she told me that she didn't care what else I did, but that it was her turn to give her granddaughter her bottle.'

Slightly winded, Anstey came up for air. 'At six o'clock?' she murmured faintly.

'It was a bit before that, I think,' Netty replied. 'But since she had that awful barney with Lester, I don't think Mrs Quartermaine sleeps all that well either.'

Anstey searched for some non-prying answer, and drew on her knowledge of the rows that had taken place in Joanna's home; and their effect on Joanna. 'Er—family—quarrels can be upsetting,' she agreed.

'I'd come that day to see Mrs Collins about something to do with the WI,' Netty said, more intent on taking Rosie from her bath and to the towel on her lap than on giving mind to what she was saying. 'I couldn't help overhearing their raised voices, and from what I heard I'd say it was more like two-sided warfare than a quarrel. Still,' she addressed Rosie, unconsciously giving her a cuddle, 'them that live the longest see the most, don't they, my beauty?'

That quaint if somewhat obscure expression gave Anstey chance to turn the conversation. She asked Netty about her Women's Institute meetings, and had the opportunity to give Rosie a cuddle herself when the baby was dressed and smelling gorgeous, and Netty handed her to her.

When Netty began tidying away, however, Anstey thought it about time that she took over. 'I'll do that,' she said, and as the thought struck, 'I can clear up here and take care of Rosie while you go and have your breakfast.'

'Gracious, I had breakfast ages ago!' Netty exclaimed, and, looking a little jealously at Rosie in Anstey's arms, 'Though I dare say they won't start breakfast downstairs until you're there.'

Oh, crikey, Anstey thought, experiencing a sudden and distinct aversion to having breakfast with Cale and his mother. Against that aversion, though, were the manners she owed to her hostess. For whatever else she had learned about the prim and proper Mrs Quartermaine, of the fact that she was fussy about manners there was no doubt.

Realising that, while she would quite well like Cale's bacon and eggs to go cold while he waited for her to join them, she had no wish for Mrs Quartermaine's breakfast fare to congeal, Anstey stood up.

'Perhaps I'd better go down,' she said, finding a smile so that Netty should not know that she would by far have preferred to miss breakfast altogether. Netty didn't need to hear more than that before she was coming forwards to take Rosie from her.

Anstey found the breakfast-room without too much trouble. As Netty had suggested, both Cale and his mother were waiting for her.

'Good morning, Mrs Quartermaine,' Anstey greeted her hostess courteously. 'I'm sorry if I'm late.'

'Good morning, Anastasia,' Mrs Quartermaine replied, as Cale left his seat and neared her guest. 'I thought you might enjoy a lie-in this morning, which is why I told Cale not to tell you what time we breakfasted.'

Not certain if Mrs Quartermaine was being kind, or if that lady too would have preferred that she missed breakfast altogether rather than join them, Anstey found that all such thoughts ceased when Cale stopped close to her. Her heart gave a jerky beat, but only from annoyance with him, she was sure. For the only reason she could see for him coming round the table was to start the day in the same way as he had ended the previous evening—with a 'lover's' kiss to her cheek.

Ready to aim a discreet kick to his shins if he so much as tried it, Anstey favoured him with hostile eyes, and endeavoured to freeze him from his objective with a cool, 'Good morning.'

'Good morning,' he replied, but the very devil was dancing in his eyes, and she felt positive that he was aware of her thoughts when he added solemnly, 'my dear,' and carried on with what he had intended doing. Courteously, he pulled out a chair for her, waited until she was seated, and then went back to his own chair.

Breakfast went better than she had anticipated. For she discovered that Mrs Quartermaine's statement that she might enjoy a lie-in stemmed only from her consideration that with a baby to look after, she must seldom have the opportunity of such luxury.

'You slept well, Anastasia?' she enquired, as Anstey consumed her usual breakfast of toast and marmalade.

'Very well, thank you,' she replied politely.

'You had no trouble getting off again—after your visit to the nursery in the small hours?' Anstey guessed that Netty had been talking.

'You went to check that the infant was all right?' Cale butted in.

'I went to feed her,' Anstey replied, taking a sip of her coffee.

'Feed her!' he exclaimed, clearly nonplussed by such goings on.

'Really, Cale!' his mother joined in. 'Surely you know that babies have to take nourishment every four hours?'

'Good God!' he muttered, and seemed so staggered that quite unexpectedly, Anstey found herself exchanging smug glances with his mother.

'Anastasia went to make Rosie's two o'clock bottle,' Mrs

Quartermaine told him with some superiority.

'Only I didn't have to,' Anstey inserted, 'because Netty had already started on it, so I went back to bed.'

'You were up again at six?' Cale cottoned on to the routine.

She shook her head. 'Netty assured me that I could trust her—and anyway,' she added with a glance at Mrs Quartermaine, 'the nursery, large as it is, might have been a trifle crowded with four of us in there.'

Cale's eyes followed hers, and they both witnessed the way Mrs Quartermaine looked momentarily startled to have been found out. And witnessed too that, although smiling, she was a touch defiant when she asked, 'And what law says that a grandmother may not feed her grand-daughter her six o'clock bottle?'

Anstey left the breakfast-room of the view that perhaps Mrs Quartermaine was not such a gorgon after all. Realising that she was feeling warmer to Cale's mother, she returned upstairs. She was beginning to see her as a more sensitive person than she had initially believed. Of course that didn't make her any less upright in her black and white high moralistic outlook, but it gave credence to her being wide open to being dreadfully hurt by her younger son's behaviour.

Anstey spent the morning in helping out in the nursery—wherever Netty would let her—but a new dimension was added to her thinking. That new dimension, her own sensitivity—towards Mrs Quartermaine.

Cale himself had said how his mother had become more and more vinegary since that row. Yet, at breakfast, she had smiled and had seemed more human. Was Rosie responsible for a thawing in that frosty lady? Was it possible that to know she was a grandmother had given Mrs Quartermaine something else to think about other than

Lester? Had Rosie's presence in the house acted as some small salve?

True, Mrs Quartermaine believed Rosie to be Cale's offspring, but she was her granddaughter just the same. Would it be so wrong to leave the baby with her for a short while? It could well further ease Mrs Quartermaine's hurt, and at the same time, Anstey cogitated, it would enable her to hold on to her job until Joanna returned ... Though what other choice did she have? Regardless of what she thought were the rights and wrongs of the issue, when it came down to basics, the plain fact was that if she didn't have a baby-minder by tomorrow morning she could look for a new job. Which would still leave her having to secure the services of a baby-minder ...

Her head had started to spin, so that Anstey was glad when Mrs Collins came to tell her that lunch was about to be served.

Anstey was in sombre mood when, a few minutes later, she descended the stairs. It was all very well to decide that, since she had to, she would leave Rosie behind, but, although Cale had been certain that his mother would offer to have her, so far Mrs Quartermaine had not done so. By the time she reached the dining-room, Anstey's only certainty was that Mrs Quartermaine would be utterly appalled if any such suggestion that she mind Rosie was put to her.

She had beaten Cale to it, Anstey saw as she entered the dining-room. Only Mrs Quartermaine was there. 'If you'd like to sit where you sat last evening,' she suggested, 'I'm sure Cale will soon be here.'

'Thank you,' Anstey murmured, and took the place her hostess had indicated, to realise with a start that it just didn't seem the same without Cale there!

Both she and Mrs Quartermaine were seated when a minute or two later he came in. By that time, though,

Anstey had perished any ridiculous notion that there was anything remotely special about him. It was just that, the mood she was in, she just wasn't up to answering—and possibly having to lie in answer to—any forthright questions which Mrs Quartermaine might put while they waited for him to appear.

'Had a good morning?' Cale enquired.

'It's been like a holiday, having a whole morning with little to do,' she replied, and picked up her spoon to start on her cold cucumber soup.

'Babies are very time-consuming, aren't they?' Mrs Quartermaine joined in the conversation.

'Extremely,' Anstey agreed, not having to lie about that.

She had not missed the thoughtful look in Mrs Quartermaine's eyes, but as the soup course ended and Mrs Collins came in with the main course, Anstey thought the subject forgotten.

Mrs Collins had gone out again, and Cale was carving the beef, though, when suddenly Mrs Quartermaine asked, 'How will you manage, Anastasia?'

'Anstey, please,' she invited, playing for time as she wondered what to make of the question. 'Thank you, Cale,' she side-stepped the question as he passed over her plate and cautioned that it was hot. But she found that Mrs Quartermaine was made of sterner stuff than to be easily put off.

'I was wondering—Anstey,' she unbent sufficiently to shorten her name, but pressed just the same, 'how you'll manage to keep on top of the career you're so keen on, while at the same time managing to see that my granddaughter has all the love and care which she needs at this precious time of her development?'

'It—might be difficult, sometimes,' Anstey replied, and wondered why, when Cale was so good at butting in, he wasn't butting in now.

'The child must not be neglected,' Mrs Quartermaine said sternly.

'She isn't,' Cale, to Anstey's relief, chipped in.

'I've seen that much for myself,' Mrs Quartermaine stated without applause. But, with her attention directed to her son, she went on, 'Just as I've seen that it's no thanks to you, Cale, that my granddaughter is so well cared for.'

'You always were a shrewd lady,' Cale complimented her, the alert look in his eyes at odds with his easy manner.

'It doesn't need too much shrewdness,' his mother volleyed back at him smartly, 'to see that you don't know one end of a baby's feeding bottle from the other. Your comments at breakfast,' she warmed to her theme, albeit her voice grew colder the more she went on, 'have made it abundantly clear that you sleep right through the night and leave this poor girl to get out of bed to feed, and to attend to, a baby who is not only her responsibility, but yours also.'

Had she not been so closely involved, Anstey thought she might well have enjoyed watching Cale getting a dressing-down. She wasn't sure about the 'poor girl' bit, though.

'Actually, Mrs Quartermaine,' without thinking, she had brought her hostess's attention back to herself as she went to deny the obvious conclusions she had drawn, 'Cale and I—we don't live together, so naturally he knows nothing about Rosie's nocturnal ...'

'You're saying,' Mrs Quartermaine interrupted, looking more askance than ever, 'that you have *sole* responsibility for the child!'

Oh, grief, Anstey thought; far from her statement that she and Cale weren't living together pleasing the older woman, it looked as though it had the opposite effect.

But she was grateful when Cale took Mrs Quartermaine's attention from her for a few minutes when, looking suitably contrite, he told her, 'I haven't been much of a

help, I admit. But I intend to change that.' Anstey gave a
start at the implication behind that last sentence, but if Cale
saw it he gave no sign. 'Anstey is most anxious to get back to
work,' he went on to explain truthfully. 'Tomorrow if
possible. But the person she wants to look after the infant
isn't available just at the moment. So,' he smiled, 'the first
thing I shall do to help Anstey when we get back will be to
put my best endeavours into assisting her to find a
temporary baby-minder for . . .'

'A baby-minder!' Mrs Quartermaine looked as horrified
as she sounded. 'You intend to push the child out until
this—professional nanny, I presume—is available to take
up her duties!'

Amazed at the construction Mrs Quartermaine had put
on what Cale had just said, Anstey could only stare when he
went on to reassure his hostile parent.

'Baby-minders are a very worthwhile group. Lots of
women would be lost without them—as Anstey will be if we
can't find one who can take the baby from about eight in
the morning until six or seven in the evening.' He then
seemed to think that no further explanation was necessary,
for, taking hold of a serving dish, he enquired, 'More
potatoes, Mother?'

Mrs Quartermaine appeared to have lost her appetite.
Anstey did only marginally better. But Cale, his appetite
unimpaired, ate sufficient to fill his frame, and seemed not
to notice how little his lunchtime companions ate.

The dessert course was underway when, having said
nothing for an age, Mrs Quartermaine suddenly broke her
silence. It was not to her son that she addressed her remarks,
however, but to Anstey.

'I've been thinking,' she said in her familiar stiff manner,
'and . . . Well, quite frankly, Ana . . . Anstey,' she corrected
herself, 'I am not at all happy at the prospect of my
granddaughter being carted through the streets of London

at dawn and at dusk, rain or shine. Nor am I happy that, regardless of whether Rosie has a slight temperature, she will be placed at risk of infection from other children who might be going down with a cold.'

Anstey had not given thought to that angle, and had no idea if ailing children were banned from a baby-minder's care. But, shaken by the outline Mrs Quartermaine had just drawn, she answered honestly, if a shade jerkily.

'I . . . I'm—not too happy—about it either.'

'Then I suggest,' Mrs Quartermaine said briskly, and detracted from any look of approval that might have escaped by inserting, '——since your career means so very much to you—that you give up this nonsense talk of taking that delightful child to strangers, and leave her here, with me.'

'I . . .' Anstey mumbled, and felt dreadful. Cale had *manipulated* his mother—and she had helped him! She felt sick inside, and was ready to confess everything. 'Mrs Quartermaine . . .' she began, her look unhappy.

'It would only be during the week,' Mrs Quartermaine said quickly, as though fearing she was about to reject her offer. 'Cale could bring you down on Friday after you've finished at your office. And it isn't as if you'd see very much of Rosie during the week, is it? By the time you got her home in the evening, it would be almost time to put her to bed, and it would save you a scramble getting both yourself and Rosie ready in the morning,' she argued, appearing so eager for her to agree, that Anstey's honesty got mixed up with her sensitivity. Helplessly, she looked to Cale for help.

'It wouldn't be too much for you?' he asked his mother seriously.

'Not a bit of it,' she scorned. 'What with the other women in this house all daft about babies—not that we'll spoil her,' she said with a quick glance to Anstey, 'I shall be lucky if I get a look in. As it is, I shall only have to whisper the word to Netty and she'll be off down the drive to pack her case to move in before I can finish. We can . . .'

'It will only be for a short while,' Anstey put in hurriedly, before Mrs Quartermaine could make her plans.

'Then—you agree?' she asked.

Anstey looked across to Cale. He met her eyes steadily, and then, almost imperceptibly, he nodded. She flicked her glance from him and back to Mrs Quartermaine. Again Anstey remembered Cale's 'Surely you can see that we, as blood relatives, can take all rights from you'.

'Yes,' she said, aware that she could give no other answer. With or without her anxiety about returning to work, Cale Quartermaine had efficiently limited her options.

Everyone appeared to be in good spirits when, later that afternoon, they said goodbye. Everyone, that was, except Anstey. Certainly Netty, with Rosie in her arms as they stood on the drive, was beaming from ear to ear. Mrs Quartermaine too had found a smile. And even Cale, as he bade his mother farewell, was, to Anstey's mind, looking pleased with himself.

'Rosie will be all right with us, I promise.' Mrs Quartermaine, perhaps noticing that Anstey didn't look exactly full of the joys of spring, came over to shake her formally by the hand. 'And you'll see her again on Friday.'

'Of course,' Anstey replied, and went to say goodbye to Netty, and to give Rosie a kiss, before going swiftly to the car.

Whether Cale sensed anything of her mood, Anstey neither knew or cared. But they had been driving silently along for about half an hour when she guessed he must have thought he had given her long enough to get over any emotional feelings about parting from Rosie. For, with an *un*emotional sideways look, he questioned conversationally, 'You're not happy about something, Anstey?'

She bit down a snappy 'I'm absolutely ecstatic about

everything' and said bluntly, 'Where would you like me to start?'

'You could try the beginning,' he offered casually, his eyes on the road ahead. 'Although, from the way events have gone, I'd have said you had small cause for complaint. You wanted someone to look after the infant,' he reminded her, 'and you've got someone to look after the infant—if I may say so, the best. You were worried about being unable to go to your job tomorrow—that worry has been taken from you. So,' he enquired, 'why so glum?'

Anstey was no more endeared to his hateful logic than she had been before. To hear him tell it, any complaint she made would be just plain bleating for the sake of it. For it was as he had said. She had needed someone to look after Rosie so that she could go to work, and he *had* taken that worry from her, though she still didn't like the way he had done it.

'If I'm glum, it's because I don't like the way you use people,' she wasted no more time to tell him. 'You were more concerned about your mother than Rosie when you took us to Quiet Ways,' she went on flatly. Not liking the weakness that dented her aggression when honesty reminded her that none of his actions had been for his own benefit, she rushed on. 'And you didn't stop there! You even manipulated your own mother into asking if she could "baby-mind" Rosie. And *I*,' she said indignantly, 'had no option but to be a party to it!'

'My word,' said Cale mildly, his tone even where hers had started to rise, 'so that's what has been stewing inside you.' He cast her another sideways glance, but had his eyes on the road again when he murmured, 'I believe I did mention on the way down that I thought my mother would volunteer to have the babe. I don't recall you raising any objection then. But,' he went on while she was hating him more because he was making it seem as if she was being unreasonable, 'I never looked on my actions today as being manipulative.'

'*You*—wouldn't!' Anstey tossed in sourly.

'From my viewpoint,' he went on, ignoring her comment, 'having spent some time with my mother this morning and being left in no doubt that Rosie Tresilla Quartermaine is the bee's knees in her opinion, I merely helped her out in what I was sure was her heartfelt longing.'

Anstey looked out of the side window to consider what he had said. She'd had a fair sample of his mother's forthright manner, and actions. Not only had she rounded on the both of them when she had seen fit, but in an attempt to push her and Cale up the altar, she had even invited the vicar to dinner. Anstey thought it most unlikely, therefore, that there was anything that Mrs Quartermaine would not say and do if she felt like it. Suddenly, though, and to give him the benefit of the doubt, Anstey remembered how after breakfast she had realised that Mrs Quartermaine was more sensitive than she had believed.

'Are you telling me,' she turned her head to ask, 'that your mother wanted me to leave Rosie with her, but that she didn't know how to ask?'

He nodded. 'She would have jumped at any opening I gave,' he stated. 'You were right when you intimated that something happens to mothers when they become grandmothers.'

'You've—noticed a change in your mother?'

'I'm still slightly stunned,' he owned. 'I'm sure she never thought twice when she engaged Netty to look after first me, and then Lester. Yet today, not taking anything away from Netty, I witnessed that she expects you to employ no one but the most highly trained professional nanny for her grandchild.'

Anstey had to smile, but her smile soon fell away. Cale had an answer for everything, but that did not make the deceit that was going on sit any more comfortably with her honest soul.

'You're still not happy, are you?' he observed when another ten minutes had silently gone by.

She shrugged. 'How can I be?' she asked tonelessly. 'It isn't right that your mother doesn't know Rosie is Lester's child. Yet, because, as you didn't hesitate to tell me, my *non*-blood tie with her makes my rights less than tenuous, I've had to go along with you and deceive your mother. Quite honestly, Cale, I don't like it.'

'Do you think I like it any better?' he asked coldly, and flicked a glance at her solemn expression, saying a trifle more warmly, 'Believe me, I appreciate and admire the honesty I've seen in you, but I've explained why it has to be this way. It's working, too,' he encouraged. 'My mother was happier today than I've seen her in a long while.'

'She—er—did smile,' Anstey agreed.

Cale grinned, 'I'm working to the day when she smiles more than she frowns, then I'll tell her that the young lady who's responsible for her smiles is still her granddaughter, but is Lester's offspring, and not mine.'

'Not before Joanna comes back!' Anstey exclaimed in sudden panic.

'You don't know where you are, do you?' Cale said softly, and actually stretched out a hand to pat one of hers in a touch of comfort. 'You're desperately torn between longing that my mother should know the truth, and at the same time being terrified that she might find out and take some action that will do away with your guardianship.'

'That,' said Anstey, touching the warm spot on her hand where his hand had rested, 'about sums it up.'

'Try not to worry,' he advised. 'You and I are in this together. I won't make a move without consulting you first.'

Anstey wasn't quite sure how she felt about being 'in' anything with Cale. He was a mixture of a man. A man

who she well knew was harder than granite, or he could
never have ruined his brother's career the way he had. Yet
he was a man who was so concerned about the inner distress
of his ageing parent that there appeared no lengths he was
not prepared to go to to secure that the rest of her life might
be spent in inner content. To say the least of it, Cale
Quartermaine was the most confusing man.

Anstey suffered more confusion when they reached
London. Without being pushy, she felt she owed it to
Joanna, if not on her own account, to go down to Quiet
Ways to see Rosie next weekend, as invited. She had still
not found a way to ask him about it when, with her
weekend case in his hand, Cale held on to it until he had
escorted her to her door, and saved her the trouble.

'I'll call for you Friday evening,' he said as he handed her
case over. And as her mouth fell slightly open, all at once
the most devilish gleam appeared in his eyes. As if her
parted lips were too much to resist, he bent his head and
lightly kissed her. 'All the best proxy-parents say farewell
like that,' he grinned, and while she just stood and stared,
and grew more confused at another facet to his character,
he turned and went cheerfully on his way.

CHAPTER SIX

THE flat seemed empty without Rosie. Anstey returned from her office on Monday evening feeling so restless that only then did she realise how attached to the baby she had become. Funnily, even though she had never taken Rosie to her place of employment, she had felt restless all through that day too.

She filled in part of the evening by having a good clear-up. But by nine o'clock, the flat looking more how it used to look, she had to admit that she had not worked the restlessness out of her spirit.

Hoping to feel more settled within herself, at ten past nine she gave in to the urge to ring Quiet Ways. Not that she had any particular wish to speak to Mrs Quartermaine, but surely, since that stately lady believed her to be Rosie's mother, she would think it only natural for her to telephone to enquire after the infant's wellbeing.

Anstey discovered that her luck was out when she was informed by directory enquiries that Mrs Quartermaine's number was ex-directory.

'Are you sure?' she asked, on the fidget within herself and not wanting to go to bed to lie awake and fidget some more.

'Quite sure,' the male operator replied. 'Sorry, love.'

Anstey came away from the phone, and exhaled a sigh. Fleetingly she thought of ringing Cale Quartermaine to ask him for his mother's telephone number. But somehow— and it had nothing to do with the memory of his lips briefly touching hers, of that she was sure—she felt reluctant to talk to him.

Needing something constructive to do, she decided to

reply to her landlord's letter. She went to bed with her reply in her bag ready to post in the morning. Without a word of a lie, she had told her landlord that although a baby had been staying in the flat, the infant was now living with her family in the country.

Anstey's restless mood followed her to work the next morning. At half past ten she realised that she was just not going to settle until she'd had a word with Mrs Quartermaine. She reached for the phone.

'Mr Quartermaine's secretary,' said a remembered voice when the telephonist at Quartermaine Holdings put her through.

'Good morning, Miss Impney,' said Anstey in business-like tone. 'I'd like to speak to Mr Quartermaine, please,' and before the efficient secretary could put the block on, 'It's Anstey Eldridge here—you may remember I came to your office last week—with Mr Quartermaine's niece.'

'I remember,' Miss Impney replied, her tone causing Anstey to think that she would never forget. 'Just a moment, please.'

'Anstey?'

'Cale,' she replied, feeling suddenly shaky but perishing the thought that he had any power to affect her whatsoever. Her voice was a shade on the cool side because of that absurd thought, when she told him, 'I need your mother's telephone number. She's not in the book.'

'What do you need her number for?' he asked curtly. 'I've already said that I'll be the one to tell her the truth when *I* feel the time is right. I've warned you . . .'

'Don't you threaten me!' Anstey flared, wondering again what it was about this man that caused her normal even temperament to be so instantly erratic. 'I merely want to ring to ask her how Rosie is,' she made herself say more evenly.

'How would she be?' he barked. 'She's fine.'

Arrogant swine! 'How do you know she's fine?' Anstey snapped, her control there only in short bursts.

'Anyone with half a brain would know that that infant is being zealously guarded by at least two women down at Quiet Ways,'

'Thank you,' Anstey snapped acidly. 'Now give a half-brained idiot that telephone number!'

'Take my word for it . . .'

'I'm not interested in your word,' Anstey cut in heatedly, too incensed that he was being obstructive purely from his cold-hearted male logic to want to bother to check her temper. 'Look here, Cale Quartermaine,' she stormed, 'I've had sole charge of Rosie for some weeks now, and not only am I missing her but, regardless of your threats, I'm still her guardian. Joanna appointed me, not you, and not your mother, and I . . .'

Cale did not allow her to finish, but sliced in to very nearly flatten her, when he challenged toughly, 'You think your claim would stand up in court?'

'What—do you mean?' she gasped.

'Precisely what I say,' he rapped. 'It was my intention, not to threaten you, but to have your co-operation over matters which I've fully explained. However,' he went on shortly, 'since you do see my remarks as a threat, then believe it—no judge would give you legal guardianship on the unwritten say-so of a woman who's deserted her child.'

'You devil!' Anstey exclaimed.

'But,' he continued, unmoved, 'it shouldn't come to that. As for you missing the infant,' he added, a new, harsher note coming to his voice, 'I can only think, from your point of view that it would be a good miss.'

'How can you say such a thing!'

'I've heard the din that mite can create,' he told her stonily. 'Her inopportune attention-seeking must have more than ruined your love-life of late.'

God! What a man! Anstey slammed the receiver down. Clearly Cale Quartermaine believed that before the arrival of Rosie, there had been fine old high jinks going on in the flat!

Anstey was still seething about Cale Quartermaine when she went home that night. Quite obviously, he thought she had lovers by the score, and that Rosie crying at an 'inopportune' moment really cramped her style. Him and his 'I can only think, from your point of view, it would be a good miss'! The way his mind worked, he no doubt thought that, with Rosie at Quiet Ways, she was all set to make up for lost time!

She had not finished fuming against him when, at around eight o'clock, there was a knock on her door. She went to open it, and nearly fell over backwards. It was him!

'In case I forgot to say it,' she bridled before he could state his business, 'the last word of my phone call was *goodbye*!' With that she would have slammed the door shut on him, but his foot was inside it before she had the chance. Then, before she knew it, so was the rest of him.

'Still the same hothead,' he remarked, as he closed the door. 'Any chance of a cup of coffee?'

If she hadn't been so shaken by his colossal nerve, Anstey might have given him explicit directions to a café a couple of streets away. As it was, she made no move to go and put the kettle on, but snapped waspishly, 'If you've come to apologise, you're wasting your time.'

'Apologise?' To her chagrin he appeared mystified about what he had to apologise for but, taking a look round the tidy flat, he commented, 'Although still a mouse-hole, this place seems larger than the last time I was here.'

'Ten out of ten for observation,' said Anstey, bridling again to hear her home referred to as a mouse-hole. 'I've put Rosie's things away for the short while until I bring her back.' He smiled. His smile worried her. 'You do know that

I shall be bringing her back?' she felt bound to press.

'You think Joanna will want her?' he enquired mildly, his answer, to Anstey's way of thinking, no answer at all.

'Of course she'll want her!' she erupted, starting to panic. Possession was said to be nine-tenths of the law! 'And no judge,' she went on shortly, combating in advance any idea the Quartermaine family might have of being obstructive, 'would dream of denying Joanna's claim to her child. Particuarly,' she stressed, 'since the child's father couldn't care two hoots what happens to her.'

'You could quite well be right,' Cale replied, but she knew she did well not to trust his insincere smile, when he added, 'although I'm not sure how any judge could decide in the mother's favour, should he learn of her unstable behaviour.'

'Unstable? Joanna's not unstable!' Anstey exclaimed, outraged.

'If you say not,' Cale shrugged, and, arrested for a moment by the angry sparks in her dark blue eyes, he went on, 'but it's hardly stable behaviour, would you say, for a mother to leave her child the way she did?'

'Joanna is not unstable,' Anstey repeated grimly. 'And it's not so much that she left her child but that, unable to take Lester's final *callous blow*, she experienced a resurgence of the compulsion to get away.'

'Resurgence?' Cale echoed, while Anstey was so worked up she was barely aware that she had said the word. 'She's done this sort of thing before?'

Oh, grief, Anstey thought, they don't come any quicker than him! 'How do you like your coffee?' she snapped; although she'd had no intention of making him coffee, her sudden desperate need for a breathing space made her head for the small kitchen.

'Black.' He followed her into the kitchen, and to her annoyance, stood close by as she set the kettle to boil.

'Sugar?' she enquired, struggling to regain her composure, her confusion having nothing at all to do with the fact that two together in the kitchen made it overcrowded

'No, thanks,' he said, and caused her heart to suddenly pound when he stretched out a hand to her face Instinctively, she ducked back. He smiled, this time a touch of amusement on his well-shaped mouth, as he merely reached over to hand her down the coffee jar.

'I'll bring it through to the sitting-room,' she said stiffly While she was not minded to invite him to take his ease suddenly it became important that he was out of the kitchen. 'If you'd like to go and take a seat,' she hinted.

Cale took the tray from her and placed it on a small table when, having absentmindedly made herself a cup of coffee as well, she joined him.

'Thank you,' she mumbled, and sat down to hand him his coffee.

'You were telling me,' he reminded her, sitting opposite her and looking every bit at ease, where she was feeling decidedly on edge, 'about Joanna's compulsion to abscond in moments of stress.'

Anstey was certain she hadn't put it like that. It amounted to the same thing, though, she realised, and was then torn between appealing to him to understand how it was with Joanna, while at the same time fearful that she might tell him too much.

'Joanna—and I,' she began slowly, 'have lived here for four years, and never once in all that time has she been so upset that she had to leave. It was only when she phoned your brother from the registrar's office, and Lester spoke to her so heartlessly, that she felt she just had to get away.

'She's been in touch with you?'

'She rang the first night asking me to keep Rosie safe for her, and said that she would need her when she returned,

Anstey told him, to let him know how much Rosie meant to Joanna.

'That was your only communication from her?' he asked, his eyes steady on hers.

'She won't ring again,' she replied, and acknowledged it for the truth. As she knew Joanna, so Joanna knew her. She would have full faith that she would keep Rosie safe—Anstey knew she could not let her down.

'You sound positive,' Cale remarked. 'Is that because her communications were limited to one phone call on her previous—departures?'

'She never rang anyone before,' Anstey told him quickly in her endeavour to show him how important Rosie must be to Joanna that she had rung this time. Too quickly, she realised with an inner groan, for she had just confirmed that at one time Joanna had made a speciality of taking flight. Clever devil, she dubbed Cale Quartermaine, too late to see that he had set a trap and she had walked straight into it. 'I told you about her spiteful stepfather,' she defended Joanna aggressively.

'He beat her?'

'He never laid a finger on her,' she denied. 'He had other methods of punishment. She was nagged from dawn to dusk. Ridiculed over any achievement. Bullied endlessly by his tongue for the slightest wrongdoing. When Joanna was too distressed to take any more, she would disappear. When she'd got herself back together, she'd return and be strong enough to take what was coming until the next time.'

'Her mother—didn't she have anything to say?'

'I think she did try to oppose him in the beginning, but when he started to give her some of the same treatment, she found it easier to say nothing. So you see,' Anstey continued to defend Joanna, 'where Lester was overindulged by his mother, Joanna was not allowed to be indulged by hers.'

Cale drank from his coffee cup, and since his expression

was hidden Anstey had no idea what he was thinking. If he was planning some fresh trap, though, she had no wish to be caught napping a second time. She decided it might be better to take the conversation completely away from Joanna. To attack might well be the answer, and it would make a nice change to see him on the defensive.

She waited only until he had put his coffee cup down, then, before he could say a word, she was in. 'Talking of indulgence,' she said coolly, 'you showed rather a lot of it, wouldn't you say, when you bought back Quiet Ways for your mother?'

His right eyebrow moved upwards a fraction, but as he sat studying her, Anstey gained an impression that he doubted that she saw his actions that way.

'I'd hardly call it an indulgence,' he remarked after a moment or two. 'Apart from a natural feeling that she shouldn't be turned out of her home, I had a duty to my father to see she is secure and as happy as she can be without him.'

Anstey's intention to attack was weakened straight away. Cale was a dutiful son, and did honour his father's memory, that much was borne out in the way he had stepped in to make sure that his mother was secure at Quiet Ways. He was prepared to go to any lengths, too, in order that his mother might again be content within herself.

In need of a spur, Anstey found the spur she needed by remembering that Mrs Quartermaine's future inner contentment lay—via Lester. That triggered off the memory of how ruthlessly Cale had ruined his brother's career.

'It's a pity,' she said tartly, 'that you didn't feel the same sense of duty towards your brother.'

For a second Cale looked surprised that, when she knew about Lester's caddish behaviour, she was suddenly going in to bat for him. But, ever a man in charge of himself, he had a trace of humour around his mouth, belied by the shrewd look in his eyes, when he replied lightly, 'I've been extracting my brother from some scrape or other since the time he was found, pullover laden with apples, in a neighbour's orchard.'

'Which is why, of course, you showed yourself so proficient at extracting him when the firm of Quartermaine Holdings was reorganised, and ...' she injected acidly ' ... you extracted him right out of his career in high finance.'

The dark frown that came to Cale's face warned her that she had overstepped the mark. But Anstey was unrepentant. 'Quite when we reorganised escapes me,' he replied evenly, 'but if my brother told you I threw him out during some reorganising exercise, then it must be true.'

'He didn't tell me, he told Jo ...' Suddenly Anstey broke off.

Had Cale attempted to defend his action, she would never have believed it had been any other than the way which, through Joanna, she had heard it. But Cale had openly agreed that he had thrown Lester out, and all at once Anstey was beginning to question something she had never thought to question before. Cale was hard, devious and a swine, but he was also honourable and knew where his duty lay ...

'You didn't reorganise—or rationalise—did you?' she asked quickly, her tone completely devoid of the acid that had been there before.

'If Lester says I did, I must have done,' he replied, his eyes on hers as she searched for answers—answers which she was starting to realise Cale wasn't readily going to give.

'I don't—believe you did,' she said slowly, and suddenly Cale's intimation that he was always extracting Lester from some scrape had fuelled the question, 'The scrape Lester got himself into when he worked for you —was one scrape too many—wasn't it?'

'You're giving me the benefit of the doubt?'

'Oh, you're a swine, a cold, calculating, devious swine, that much I realise,' Anstey replied, 'but you do know where your duty lies. You bought back Quiet Ways for your mother when Lester borrowed money from . . .' On a gasp, Anstey's voice petered out. Suddenly she was remembering Joanna telling her how Lester's position in Quartermaine Holdings gave him authority to sign the company's cheques. 'He borrowed from—Quartermaine Holdings—didn't he?'

Several seconds passed while Cale just looked at her, then, with a murmured, 'I never *did* consider you half-brained,' he left his chair and headed towards the door.

'He—embezzled money from Quartermaine Holdings!' Anstey croaked, as it slotted into place in her head, and she left her chair too, to go to the door with Cale.

He was standing but a step away when he halted at the door and looked down at her. 'Lester called it borrowing,' he muttered, 'but the stockholders would have used your word had I been unable to put things right.'

'Oh, Cale,' she said, and suddenly she realised that he must be fond of his brother, and that Lester's actions had hurt more than Cale's pockets. 'I'm so sorry.'

'Don't be,' Cale smiled, and stretched out a hand to tap her lightly on the nose. 'Sorrow wasn't what I felt,' he told her.

'You were angry?'

Cale's gaze became fixed on the rarity of a warm look from her. 'I was as mad as hell,' he said. 'I handle other people's money, and any standing I have in the city comes from the cast-iron integrity the name Quartermaine has established over the years. When I discovered what Lester, a Quartermaine, had been up to, I threw him out without caring a damn what happened to him.'

'You couldn't have done anything else,' Anstey murmured, oddly her skin still tingling from the feel on Cale's
forefinger on the tip of her nose.

'So you don't see me as such a villain?' he smiled.

Anstey smiled back, but as she realised that she liked his
gentle smile, she suddenly became aware that she was in
danger of being totally disarmed. She made great efforts to
counter that situation.

'Er—why did you call, by the way?' she asked, the cool
note she was after not quite coming off. 'It wasn't just for a
cup of coffee?' she tried again.

His smile again disarmed her. 'I spoke to my mother
about the infant,' he said, to dent her efforts some more as
she realised he could not be entirely insensitive to her
telling him that she was missing the baby. 'Rosie, by all
accounts, is a little treasure. She's guzzling her bottles as fast
as Netty can make them and, although given to tantrums
when she wants to be noticed, she has a smile, according to
my mother, that would charm the birds from the trees. In
other words,' said Cale, 'that yelling bundle is adored and
flourishing.'

Any feelings of disquiet Anstey felt that Mrs Quartermaine might be growing too attached to Rosie were
overshadowed by her wonder that Cale was more sensitive
than she had believed. No man who was purely as hard as
she had thought him would have gone out of his way to
telephone Quiet Ways on her behalf. Nor, ignoring the
facility of the telephone, would any insensitive man call in
person to tell her the result of his enquiries about Rosie.

'You're kind,' tripped off her tongue before she could
stop it.

'So,' said Cale, bending to plant a light kiss to her cheek,
'are you. I'll go further,' he added as he straightened.
'You're not only kind, but to do all you have for your friend

makes you a very exceptional person.'

Anstey knew he was about to leave, and she moved nearer, intending to open the door. 'We're in danger of becoming a mutual admiration society,' she laughed.

'We can't have that,' he agreed, and reached down for the door handle at the same time that she did. A tingle went all the way up her arm as their fingers touched, and she went to pull her hand back. But Cale had her hand in his and was still holding it when, some emotion in his eyes which she did not understand, he said throatily, 'Dammit, Anstey, I've got to kiss you ...'

She had no objection to make when he did just that. In fact, as he gathered her into his arms, she moved to him. When his lips met hers, her hands were on his shoulders. Gently at first, he kissed her.

He broke his kiss to look into her eyes. She smiled a little shyly, but did not hold back when he read her smile as encouragement and kissed her again. Time passed her by as his ardour increased and the gentleness of his first kisses gave way to passion.

When, many kisses later, his lips left hers, and he kissed her eyes, then trailed kisses down to her throat, such a fire entered her being that, although there was an instinctive part of her that always backed off near that point, this time that instinct was nowhere to be seen.

'I want you, my dear,' Cale murmured hoarsely, and Anstey for her part, did not want him to stop. Her answer was to press herself to him, the better to feel his vibrant male warmth.

Cale kissed her again, his mouth teasing her lips apart, and her heart thudded excitedly against her ribs. A fire scorched the whole of her being, and she had little comprehension of what she had committed herself to when Cale gently eased her up and carried her into the bedroom.

In a world she had never been in before, she was still not

capable of thinking, only of glorying, when, with Cale close with her on the single mattress of her bed, they lay together.

Shyness smote her when he unbuttoned her dress and began to remove it. But she thrilled to the feel of his hands on her body.

'Your skin's like silk,' he murmured, and caused her only to want to feel what his skin was like to touch.

He helped her when her trembling fingers had difficulty in unbuttoning his shirt. 'Oh, Cale,' she sighed, and wanted to feel his hair-roughened chest against her.

Voluntarily she gave him her lips, and she closed her eyes. Half lying over her, he took her to new heights. Where her bra had gone, she neither knew nor cared; just the feel of his mouth, gentle as he traced kisses down to her naked breasts, was rapture.

'I've got to have you, Anstey,' he whispered. 'Is it the same with you?'

'Yes, oh yes,' she moaned, and knew more rapture when, as he kissed a pulse spot behind her ear, his body came over hers and, as if the feel of her breasts under him was driving him slightly insane, he brushed his chest gently over them.

She had her eyes closed when his body pulled away. She opened her eyes and was ready to beg him to come closer to her again. 'Oh, God,' he groaned, 'I want you. I want you—now,' and with that, Anstey realised why he had moved a little from her.

She saw his hands go down to the remaining item of clothing he had on. Quickly, as her instinct to back off belatedly gave her a nudge, she averted her eyes. She never afterwards knew whether she would have made complete love with Cale or not.

But as she averted her eyes, her glance fell on the photograph which she had replaced on the table between her bed and Joanna's. The back of the picture frame was towards her, but the photograph of Joanna and Lester, so

much in love, was for ever imprinted on her mind. And all
Anstey knew then was that what she was about to do was
wrong. Joanna and Lester had the excuse of love for having
been lovers as they had. She did not love Cale, and he did
not love her. What motivated them was nothing but—*lust*!

'I . . .' she began, and was suddenly dreadfully alarmed
that she had left it too late.

Terrified that Cale would not take no for an answer,
Anstey shot from the bed. In one movement she had
grabbed the top cover from Joanna's bed, and covering
herself as she went, she went flying into the sitting-room.

When, some minutes later, a fully dressed Cale joined
her, Anstey was still trembling. Yet while one half of her
seemed to want to apologise for her behaviour, the other
half of her wanted to attack him for having been able to
make such a nonsense of her.

Cale did not look pleased, she noticed when she flicked a
quick glance to his face and away again. Nor did he sound
it when, as he made for the door, he tossed in her direction,
'I'll say this for you—you sure as hell know how to tease.'

'It w-wasn't—deliberate,' she said shakily. 'I didn't
m-mean to . . .'

He was at the door when, sending her a no-love-lost look,
he snarled, 'Get your act together, sweetheart. Either you
want a—bedroom romp—or you don't!'

Anstey guessed he had used the words 'bedroom romp' to
be deliberately insulting. And she was insulted that he
could talk so about what, up until almost the last, had been
a new and enchanting experience for her. Well, two could
play at the insults game.

'A "bedroom romp" would have suited me just fine,
sweetheart!' she drawled. 'Only just in time my eyes caught
the photograph of your brother and my best friend. I
realised then that, should I become pregnant, you'd act no
better with me than Lester acted with Joanna. You'd be all

for an abortion too—wouldn't you?'

The slam of the door was the only answer she received, though Anstey had read enough in his outraged expression to know that he had only left to save himself from throttling her.

Admitting half an hour later that she was still somewhat confused by all that had taken place, Anstey was clear in her head about one thing. Cale Quartermaine had objected strongly to being tarred with the same brush as his brother.

She thought her confusion had cleared a little by the time she took herself off to bed. But then she realised that she could not be so clear-headed as she had thought. Because somehow the notion would not leave her mind that, whatever else Cale Quartermaine was, he was the complete opposite of, and a better man than, his brother.

CHAPTER SEVEN

By Friday, Anstey had been through a whole range of emotions. She was still missing Rosie, but the absence of the baby gave her more than enough time to dwell on Cale Quartermaine.

She found it most disturbing the way thoughts of him would so frequently pop into her head. At the briefest lull he would be there. Sometimes, even when she would be working flat out at the office, a memory of him would shoot into her head to break her concentration.

She tried hard not to remember their passionate lovemaking, but it was not easy. Time and again she would feel her body grow hot with mortifying heat as she remembered how, completely without protest, she had allowed him to carry her to her bedroom!

Never had she known that she was capable of acting like that. She suffered more mortification when she recalled how eagerly she had welcomed, and responded to, Cale's ardent kisses and caresses. Dear heaven, what had come over her?

Anstey went out at lunch time that Friday and decided that she still didn't like Cale Quartermaine any better. Any man who could cold-heartedly reduce what for her had been a shattering experience to the level of a 'bedroom romp' didn't deserve to be liked.

She returned from her lunch to know some slight confusion, when the honesty in her soul made her question what else he should call it. The only reason she had bolted off the bed the way she had had been the sudden realisation that the only thing that had motivated either of them was lust.

Fed up with Cale Quartermaine being for ever in her head, Anstey concentrated on her work, and re-endorsed how much she hated him. She now realised, of course, that he was not quite the villain Lester had painted him, but that was by the way.

He had said he would call for her this evening to take her down to Quiet Ways, but when Anstey recalled his outraged expression when he had left her flat last Tuesday, she calculated that she hadn't better hold her breath waiting for his knock.

In her surmise, though, that if she wanted to go down to see Rosie at Quiet Ways that weekend she would be going under her own steam, she was proved wrong. It was at around half past four when the phone on her desk rang. She picked it up.

'Miss Eldridge?' enquired a female voice that was vaguely familiar.

'Speaking,' she answered.

'Lucy Impney,' her caller identified herself. 'Mr Quartermaine has asked me to ring. His meeting is over-running, so he won't be able to call for you until some time after eight.'

'Thank you, Miss Impney,' Anstey answered evenly, and replaced the phone to come to the startling awareness that she was smiling.

Oh, good grief, she thought in self-disgust, anybody would think I'm ecstatic to have confirmation that I'm to see that cold-hearted swine again! The excited flutter she felt in the region of her heart had nothing to do with him either. Who wouldn't be excited at the prospect of seeing little Rosie again?

Anstey had her weekend case packed and was ready and waiting for Cale at eight o'clock. She owned to feeling a trifle embarrassed at the prospect of the initial minutes of their meeting. For it wasn't every day, or ever, for that matter, that she lay near-naked in a man's arms, mindless to everything but him.

It was that embarrassment, she realised, which was the cause for the energetic bumping in her heart when, fifteen minutes later, she heard him coming up the stairs. She picked up her case, adopted a cool front, and went to the door.

'Good evening,' she said coolly, too busy inserting her key in the outside of her door to look at him.

A grunt was her reply as, taking her case from her hand, Cale left her to lock up the flat, and went to wait in the car.

'Have you eaten?' he enquired uninvitingly as he pulled the car away from the kerb. 'I've told my mother not to wait dinner for us.'

'I've eaten,' Anstey replied. It was about the sum total of their conversation on the journey to Quiet Ways.

No sooner had Cale opened the front door and escorted her into the hall of his mother's home, though, than Anstey stopped dead. There, under the arch of the staircase, stood the very Rolls-Royce of a baby-carriage.

Her eyes were still riveted to the colossally expensive pram when Mrs Quartermaine, obviously having heard them arrive, came into the hall to greet them.

'I hope you don't mind, Ana ... Anstey,' she said on observing that Anstey was having difficulty in dragging her eyes away from the baby-carriage. 'But when we did manage to get those fold-away wheels you left attached to the carry-cot, we found that pushing it over the gravel drive gave little Rosie too bumpy a ride when we took her out for her airings.'

Dearly did Anstey wish that Mrs Quartermaine had not gone to the trouble. It would be a totally wasted expense when she took Rosie back to the flat, because there would be no room to house it—Kenneth Davies would have a fit if she suggested leaving it in the hall.

'It's—a beautiful pram,' she told Mrs Quartermaine truthfully, and kept her feelings of disquiet to herself.

'Would you like supper?' her hostess asked as they walked along the hall.

'I don't know about Cale,' Anstey said, suddenly realising that he was looking at her, and that, although not saying anything, he was taking everything in, 'but I'm not hungry. Actually,' she said, pausing as they reached the bottom of the stairs, 'I thought I'd just pop in to see Rosie, and then go to bed.'

'Of course,' Mrs Quartermaine replied, and as she halted in a better light Anstey noticed how, in less than a week, years seemed to have fallen away from Cale's mother. 'I expect,' she went on civilly, 'that you put so much effort into your career that you're exhausted by Friday. You're in the same room as last time,' she added and just as Anstey was about to go up the stairs, 'You—er—won't disturb Rosie if she's asleep, will you?' she asked, and caused Anstey to feel disturbed that even though Mrs Quartermaine believed her to be Rosie's mother, she was not letting go her temporary guardianship of the baby.

'No,' she said quietly, and went up the stairs.

Rosie was wide awake when Anstey went into the nursery, and for a change, was full of smiles. 'She's been as good as gold all week, haven't you, my lovely.' Netty, in her adoration, stretched the truth a mile, and placed Rosie in Anstey's arms.

'I'm sure she has,' Anstey replied, not believing it for a minute unless Rosie had undergone a drastic change of temperament. 'She's grown, too,' she observed, 'I'm sure she has.'

Netty took that as a personal compliment, and announced with some pride that the baby had actually started to sleep through the night, though she did qualify that Rosie had only done it once.

Anstey was not happy when she went to bed that night, though she had to admit that the baby was blossoming down at Quiet Ways. As Cale had said, Rosie was flourishing, so she had no argument on that score—but had she done the right thing to bring her here?

She was still in a worried frame of mind when she went along to the nursery the next morning. Rosie was contentedly asleep, but Anstey found more cause for anxiety when she saw the clothes which Netty was getting ready for when Rosie had had her bath.

'Where did all these come from?' she asked, looking past Netty into the open airing cupboard full of baby clothes, none of which she recognised.

'Mrs Quartermaine went into Winchester on Wednesday and had a lovely time,' Netty told her enthusiastically. 'Did you see the pram in the hall.'

'It's a beauty,' Anstey murmured, and went down to breakfast with the feeling that her guardianship of Rosie was getting away from her.

She managed to raise a smile to greet Mrs Quartermaine, and received her apologies that Cale had breakfasted earlier because he had gone to see a builder who was giving her a hard time because she would not pay his bill until he did his repair work properly.

'You've seen Rosie this morning?' Mrs Quartermaine continued, and caused Anstey some more disquiet when the rest of the meal-time conversation was entirely about Rosie.

Anstey was getting seriously worried when she returned to the nursery after breakfast. She helped out where she could, but she could not get off her mind her observations that already Mrs Quartermaine had grown *too* attached to the baby.

'I'll take Rosie out for an airing, if you like,' she told

Netty when Rosie was eventually fed and bathed, and dressed in a beautifully smocked dress. But any hope Anstey had, as she pushed the plush pram down a country lane, of perhaps leaving her worries back at Quiet Ways, proved barren.

The problem of her being able to return to work had been solved, but at what cost? Suddenly she realised that she had no wish to add to the hurt Mrs Quartermaine had suffered. Yet against that, Joanna had suffered too.

Guilt came also to plague Anstey. It was too late now to have regrets, but she should never have brought Rosie to Quiet Ways. The very fact that Joanna was staying away so long surely meant that she was determined not to return until she had Lester completely out of her system? Which in turn made it more than certain that when she did come home, she would be dead-set against her daughter having anything to do with the Quartermaine family.

Anstey returned to the house only when good manners reminded her that Mrs Quartermaine would view with disfavour any guest absent from the lunch table without prior notification. She returned Rosie to Netty, and felt more depressed than ever. All she could see that she had done for Joanna was to give her more problems than she'd had before she went away.

After a quick visit to her room to tidy her hair and wash her hands, she went down to the dining-room. Cale was already there, and so was his mother. He seemed in a more affable mood than he had been the previous evening, but Anstey had too much on her mind to want to enter into any sort of conversation.

'How did your morning go?' he enquired, his manner pleasant, but his eyes sharp on her solemn expression.

'Fine, thank you,' she replied, and concentrated on what she should do now. Mrs Quartermaine was a lady of strong opinions, and, leaving aside her obvious enchantment with

Rosie, she would see it as her right to have some say in her granddaughter's upbringing. Belatedly Anstey realised that Joanna, who could be equally strong-minded, as she had shown by not letting her own mother know about the baby, would most likely be furious that her daughter had been introduced to her other grandmother, and might vow to never let her see her again. Hindsight, Anstey thought unhappily, was a terrible burden. But either way, somebody was going to be dreadfully hurt before all this business was over. She didn't want it to be Mrs Quartermaine, nor did she want it to be Joanna. Both had suffered enough.

'More cheesecake, Anstey?'

Anstey was brought away from the strain of her thoughts to realise that Mrs Quartermaine was addressing her.

'Er—no, thank you,' she replied, and looked down to her plate to see that barely a crumb of cheesecake remained. It was rather startling to awaken to the fact that she must have chewed and swallowed her way through a three-course meal without being aware of what she had eaten, or that she had eaten at all.

'*I* usually give Rosie her two o'clock bottle. Do you mind?' Mrs Quartermaine, smiling and quite clearly looking forward to the event, knocked another nail in the coffin of Anstey's despair.

'Not at all,' she answered, and watched unhappily as that lady, not waiting for coffee, went in a sprightly manner from the room.

Anstey decided that she did not want coffee either. But having decided to leave the table, she had only folded up her napkin when Cale was asking,

'What's wrong?'

She sent him a cross look. 'What's right?' she answered belligerently.

Cale ignored her cross expression, just as he ignored her

belligerent attitude. 'I told you once before that I'm prepared to help,' he reminded her evenly.

'I accepted a basinful of your help once before,' Anstey told him tartly. 'And look where that got me!'

'You're regretting that you were able to return to your job last Monday?' he queried.

Anstey considered that was a low punch. 'I'm regretting that I allowed myself to be talked into bringing Rosie here for your mother to baby-mind for me,' she snapped, and had another helping of his loathsome logic, when he replied calmly.

'Surely everything's working out as I said it would?'

'It's what you didn't say that's the trouble,' she flared. 'Given that you've more cunning than a cart-load of monkeys, and had very different reasons from purely wanting to take an avuncular share of the responsibility for Rosie—as I, *innocently*, supposed—you might have warned me that your mother would think only the best is good enough for her granddaughter.'

'You're referring to that chariot in the hall?'

'And other things.'

'Dear me, Anstey,' he drawled, 'you are in a state. I assure you,' he went on placatingly, 'that my mother can well afford that item I barked my shins on when I came in.'

Anstey refused to feel guilty that perhaps she hadn't parked the pram in quite the same spot where she had found it. She refused also to be placated, and she hoped his shins still hurt.

'It's not just the pram, nor the complete new wardrobe your mother has rigged Rosie out with,' she told him heatedly. 'She's getting too attached to Joanna's baby! Rosie's been here barely a week, yet already she dominates the whole of your mother's conversation.'

'That's all to the good, surely,' Cale countered. 'You must have seen how much less careworn my mother's looking since she's had the infant to concentrate on. And at least when we return to London tomorrow, you'll be able to rest easy that the child is not only being well cared for, but is loved.'

'That's just the point!' snapped Anstey. 'Your mother is so taken with her that soon she'll be so attached to her that she won't want to let her go! Joanna's going to love that, isn't she?' she stormed on, the worries she had nursed all that morning finding release in a sudden burst of fury. 'What the dickens do you think Joanna's going to say when she comes home to no baby, and asks what I've done with her? She'll ...'

'She should have been more concerned about what you would do at the outset, when she left the child in your charge,' Cale, his calm tone gone, cut in sharply. 'Had she any concern whatsoever for the product of her liaison with my brother,' he went on bluntly, 'she would never have left her with you, a non-relation,' he inserted. 'She must have had some idea of the difficulties you would experience. Yet only once has she seen fit to telephone you.'

'I've explained all that!' Anstey took exception to his tough remarks, and came out fighting. 'Had your brother not told her he loved her, used her, and then walked out on her, *and*,' she underlined, 'then had the appalling heartless ness to kick her when she was down and as good as deny that he was Rosie's father, then Joanna would never have gone away. As it is,' she went on, not finished yet, 'she *ha* gone away. And I, her best friend, her sister but for the blood which you haven't hesitated to remind me we *don'* share, have done a wonderful job in keeping Rosie safe for her, haven't I?'

'I consider you have,' Cale replied, calm again, even a trace of a smile around his mouth as he looked at her.

'Oh, sure!' Anstey flared. 'What better way could I look after Rosie than to bring her into the enemy camp!' Sh ignored the lift of his right eyebrow at her terminology, and ploughed on. 'The longer Rosie stays with Lester's family, the more entrenched your mother's attachment becomes. Heaven knows what Joanna will say when she gets back, but if she doesn't return soon, then Lester's family will be taking over the baby . . .' Anstey finally started to run out of steam, ' . . . and from where I'm sitting,' she finished, suddenly more fed up than ever, 'there seems to be little I can do to prevent it.'

Her flurry of anger spent, she noticed the thoughtful light that came into Cale's eyes. She took her glance from him, to stare dejectedly down at the pristine table cloth. Cale had once said that the situation was a mess. He had twice said that he was prepared to help. She had declined his second offer of help purely because since it had become a worse mess than ever, there was very little he could do to help anyway.

She had to give him full marks, however, when, just as she was deciding that she might as well go up to her room as to sit there waiting for him to come up with anything brilliant—he did just that. Though in her view, it was more shaking than brilliant.

'You could,' he said, and waited until she raised her head to look at him, then added, quite seriously, 'marry me.'

Anstey supposed it was natural that her heart should take a sudden leap to hear such a suggestion. It wasn't every day that she received a proposal. Though her heartbeat soon settled down when she realised that, whatever else was behind his astonishing proposal, it certainly wasn't love. Cale's bland expression told her that much. She had rather fancied that when some man voiced that particular question to her, he might wait with some tension for her answer. There was no such tension in Cale's expression. If he'd just suggested 'Shall we take the dog for a walk?' she supposed he might wear the same take-it-or-leave-it expression. But he said nothing more after this astonishing proposal, which was sufficient for her to realise that he expected some sort of an answer. She gave him one.

'And what,' she scorned, 'would my marrying you, a confirmed bachelor, achieve?'

'You would achieve the only thing that concerns you, my dear Anstey,' he drawled casually. 'If you were a member of my family—as a Quartermaine—your right to have a say in what goes on with regard to the infant would be firmly established.'

Anstey sorely needed that right. The way she saw it, the longer Joanna stayed away, the more the rights Joanna had invested in her seemed to be slipping away from her. But she was getting to know Cale Quartermaine, and she had suficient experience of how devious he could be to be wary. She had no intention of taking him up on his offer, but her acquaintance with his 'come into my parlour' tactics was enough to make her question the real motive behind that offer.

'And what,' she asked coolly, 'do you get out of it?' Cale eyed her seriously, but his delay in answering straight away gave her time to remember how on Tuesday, his voice hoarse with desire, he had told her that he wanted her. 'Dear me, Cale,' she gibed when he had still not answered 'marriage is a bit of a drastic step, wouldn't you say—just to satiate the lust you have for my body?'

To her chagrin, Cale was unmoved by her gibe, and she was the one to feel uncomfortable when, with a flicker glance down to her breasts, he replied, 'Beautiful as I recall your body is, I'm more concerned with getting my mother off my back than with satiating any passing lust—which, as I recall, was mutual at the time.' Anstey wished desperately that she could deny what he said, but he was going on 'Contrary to your opinion that she can think and talk of nothing but her grandchild, my mother's been on the phone to me every day this week, pressing that I do the "right" thing, and marry you.'

Oh, help—she had believed that Mrs Quartermaine had accepted that she and Cale did not wish to marry, but apparently, she had never let up on that score for a second! But Anstey was still feeling the sting of Cale's words on the subject of his 'passing' lust, and it didn't take her long to have an answer for him.

'There's an easy way to get your mother off your back,' she tossed at him. 'All you have to do is tell her the truth. Tell her that you're not Rosie's father, and . . .'

'If I did that,' Cale cut in coolly, 'I should also have to tell her that you are not Rosie's mother. I know my parent well,' he went on pleasantly. 'Believe it, she wouldn't wait to hear much more than that before she'd be off to her lawyers to have the child legally assigned to her full care—pending adoption.'

Anstey blanched, but even as she gasped, 'She wouldn't!' she knew that he was speaking the truth.

'She would,' Cale replied levelly.

'Oh, lord,' Anstey groaned and, having had more than she could take for the time being, she got up and left him.

Instinctively she went towards the staircase. At the bottom of the stairs, she changed her mind and turned about. Both Mrs Quartermaine and Netty would be in the nursery. Too upset just then to want to go to her room only to pace the floor, Anstey headed out into the sunshine.

Her walk took her along the road she had wheeled Rosie along that morning, and at first her thoughts were a jumble. Gradually though, her inner turmoil evened out, and her thinking became clearer.

She had no idea if Mrs Quartermaine would be allowed to legally adopt Rosie, or if she wouldn't. But it was odds on, apart from the blood-tie, that when it came to the financial aspect, the baby's grandmother would be more favoured in court than her own impecunious self.

Anstey fell to wondering where Joanna was, and wished with all her heart that she would come home. But it was ground she had been over time and time again, and so far, for all of her wishing, Joanna was still not back.

Leaving the futility of wishing, Anstey began to think of things which she had pushed to the back of her mind. It was then that she realised she must have been off her head to have credited Cale Quartermaine with any sensitivity. He hadn't telephoned his mother because she was missing the baby! His mother had telephoned him! In all probability, the only reason he'd mentioned Rosie at all was in an endeavour to get his mother off the subject she was insistent on bending his ear with—that subject—marriage.

Anstey felt most peculiar inside when she thought of the way Cale had, in effect, asked her to marry him. But some obstinate streak refused to allow her to dwell on his proposal. Instead she thought of all she disliked about him. How she hated his logic, his deviousness, and his lack of sensitivity.

Somehow, though, her concrete opinion that he hadn't an ounce of sensitivity suddenly began to crumble. Without any awareness of the path her thoughts had started to travel, she began to remember his loyalty to his family. Lester had 'borrowed' money from Cale and Mrs Quartermaine, criminally in one case, if not in both. Yet Cale had been reluctant to say a word against him. Infuriated by Lester a second time, he had even swallowed his fury to go and see him when he'd seen how Lester's continued absence from Quiet Ways was affecting his mother.

And, even if Cale had not specifically telephoned to ask after Rosie, was it the act of an insensitive man to put himself out and call in person at her flat last Tuesday, to tell her that Rosie was flourishing?

It was not the first time Anstey remembered Cale's visit to her flat, so she had no trouble in remembering that she had thought him kind then, and had even told him so. She remembered too how she had warmed to him. And how, before he had left, she had experienced a new and a different kind of warmth.

Quite startlingly then, she received the biggest jolt of all. Because suddenly, in thinking of his kisses and his kindness, quite without warning, she knew that she wanted more of his kisses, more of his kindness. Just like that, without any sense to it whatsoever, Anstey realised that, quite irrevocably, she was in love with Cale Quartermaine.

Stunned, she went and leant against a five-barred gate without being aware even that there *was* a five-barred gate on that stretch of country road.

The how, the why and the when of her coming to fall in love with him were obscure to her. But, staggered by her new-found knowledge, she could only suppose it had started from the moment she had first clapped eyes on him. From the start he had evoked emotion in her, be that emotion fury or whatever. But from the beginning she had been far from impervious to him.

Anstey did not have to question the new and powerful emotion which she had only just recognised. She had put up a barrier of hate, but that barrier had come crashing down. She loved him, was in love with him, and however painful that love might be she had to face the fact that love was not something you could turn off at will.

Eventually she came away from the gate, and turned towards Quiet Ways, her head full of Cale. She went over conversations with him, and remembered all that he had said, all that he had done. And when she came to remembering how he had suggested that she should marry him, she realised why, a short while ago, she had refused to dwell on his astounding proposal. Her heart must have

known then that she was in love with him, while her head
was having a last-ditch stand not to allow that fact to see
daylight. Because deep down, both heart and head had
known that there was nothing she wanted more than to
marry Cale Quartermaine.

Her love for him uppermost, it was as her heartbeat
started to race that she found she was wondering—why
shouldn't she marry him? He *had* asked her, after all,
and ... Her heartbeat evened out to a slow dull tempo.
Cale's proposal had not been motivated by love, but
stemmed only from weariness with his mother's phone calls.
More than likely Mrs Quartermaine rang him at his office
at a time when she knew he would be at his most busy. From
what she knew of him, Anstey realised that he would be too
courteous to his mother to have her informed that he was
not available. After a week of persistent phone calls, Anstey
could well see Cale being ready to propose anything, if it
would stop his mother from so constantly interrupting his
work. As he said, he knew his parent well, so he must have
realised that only if he were able to tell her that he had
proposed marriage would she allow him to get on with the,
to him, more important matter of running his business.

Torn in two, Anstey dressed for dinner that night, dearly
wanting to run away and leave them all to it. For Joanna's
sake, though, she had to stick it out and keep up the
pretence that she was Rosie's mother.

She left her room and was about to go downstairs when
suddenly the thought of sitting across the table from Cale
brought on a mixture of excitement and nerves. Without
thinking, she ducked into the nursery.

'Everything all right?' she asked Netty.

'Couldn't be better,' Netty beamed.

With not even a mini-crisis to delay her, Anstey said she
would look in later, and left her to it. On the way to the
dining-room she gave herself the sternest lecture on how

Cale must not be allowed to see so much as a glimmer of how she felt about him.

The aloof front she had just decided to adopt proved unnecessary. For no sooner was dinner under way than it became apparent that Mrs Quartermaine had a great deal on her mind. Fortunately she addressed her remarks to her son, but Anstey was left in the uncomfortable role of silent bystander.

She had hardly started on her smoked salmon when Mrs. Quartermaine looked at Cale and, as if it had been stewing away inside her, went into the attack. 'What exactly,' she challenged straight from the shoulder, 'do you intend to do about your daughter?'

Anstey realised then as she glanced at her hostess's severe expression that, having been fobbed off by him all week, Mrs Quartermaine was determined to have some answers.

She had been careful not to let her eyes linger on Cale for too long, but his delay in answering his mother caused Anstey to flick a glance to him. From the serious expression he wore she gathered that he too had recognised that his parent meant business, and guessed that he was weighing up the most tactful reply.

'Naturally,' he said after what had seemed minutes, but which was probably only seconds, 'I shall make provision for your granddaughter.'

He was tucking into his salmon when Mrs Quartermaine told him coldly, '*That* is not what I meant.'

Anstey was certain that Cale knew exactly what she had meant. But just in case he didn't, Mrs Quartermaine spent the time until Mrs Collins came in to clear away their plates enlightening him.

Nor did she lose track of her subject when, the second course served, Mrs Collins departed. On and on she went about the dishonour he had brought to the name of

Quartermaine, her central point being her grand-daughter's illegitimacy.

The more she piled the pressure on, the more Anstey's appetite dwindled, until suddenly her love for Cale rose up and her heart began to ache for the hammering he was taking. Time and time again she had to bite her tongue not to intervene.

Cale's replies to his mother were always courteous, but it was still going on when Mrs Collins came in with the last course. There was a brief lull until she went out again, then Mrs Quartermaine started off once more.

Anstey came near to saying something when Mrs Quartermaine made reference to her in the context that many women coped with marriage *and* a career, but somehow she managed to stay quiet.

She had quickly realised that by refusing to reveal that the baby was the offspring of neither of them Cale was defending her rights regarding Rosie. But the more he was forced to take to defend her rights, the more Anstey had to restrain the urge to jump in and defend—him.

'Is Rosie to grow up to be told that she is illegitimate?' Mrs Quartermaine questioned forthrightly, her temper starting to fray when she appeared to be getting nowhere.

'She'll be told when the time is right for her to be told,' Cale answered evenly.

'You think there is a *right* time for a child to be told that sort of thing!' Mrs Quartermaine erupted angrily. 'You're prepared to shatter her happy world when she starts to attend school, only to wonder why her school companions snigger behind her back?'

'I haven't made any decision about her schooling yet.'

'But she will go to school,' his mother said tightly, 'and since there's always one spiteful girl in the class, I hope you'll be ready when she comes to you one day breaking her heart over what has been said to her.'

Anstey felt as if her own heart was breaking, but Cale remained courteous as he replied, 'I hope I will be.'

Mrs Quartermaine tried another tack—emotional blackmail—on her own account. 'Obviously you aren't worried about the trauma the child will suffer—but have you no thought for me?'

Cale seemed suddenly stuck to know how to answer that one, and Anstey, with so much love in her heart for him, felt it almost like a physical pain that while he was doing all he could to prevent his mother taking over Rosie's guardianship, she was saying nothing. Unable to stay quiet any longer, she opened her mouth to say something, anything. But before she could go to his defence, he had found the words to stall.

'In—what connection?'

'Have you no thought to how I'm going to feel when I introduce Rosie as my granddaughter, and people exclaim, "I didn't know you had a married son!"?'

'I . . .' Cale began, but when he again seemed to be stuck for words—words sprang from Anstey.

Her heart wrenched, she just couldn't take any more. Words left her, words which she didn't know she was going to say, words which she hadn't meant to say. But words which, in her defence of the man she loved, just seemed to leap from her of their own volition.

'Actually, Mrs Quartermaine,' she heard her voice say clearly, 'Cale has asked me to marry him, and I've accepted him.'

Suddenly—the room was hushed.

CHAPTER EIGHT

HAD she really said that? Had she really said that Cale had asked her to marry him, and that she had accepted his proposal? Aghast, Anstey did not dare to look at him.

One quick look at Mrs Quartermaine, though, was all that was needed for her to know that she had indeed said what she had! Gone was the severe and angry expression her hostess had worn. Suddenly her face was wreathed in smiles as she turned to her son. Anstey found her pudding plate of great interest.

'You wicked man!' Mrs Quartermaine scolded Cale with mock severity. 'You've been stringing me along for pure devilment! You let me go on as I did, when all the time you have this wonderful news ready to tell me!'

'I couldn't resist it,' he replied, but Anstey was in shock, and save for vaguely recognising that he was not denying anything of her statement, she had no idea what else was said between mother and son.

Oh, what had she done? She hadn't meant to say what she had! She hadn't! She hadn't! Mortified, and wanting the floor to open up, Anstey could only gather that her love for Cale had not come alone. Inbuilt with that love, part and parcel of it, was an instinct that pushed her to take on all comers if he was under attack.

While another instinct must have been at work telling her not to give away to Mrs Quartermaine the fact that Rosie was not her daughter, it was an instinct interwoven in her love for Cale which had surfaced a few minutes ago and had seen her go to his defence and so crazily say what she had.

Shaken, she wondered for a confused moment if her subconscious had run away with her tongue because it knew, as she did, that she would like to marry Cale above all else. But, too stricken to have a word to say for herself, though she reckoned she had just said more than enough, she was jerked from her stab at self-analysis by realising that Mrs Quartermaine was leaving the table.

Oh, no! She couldn't be left alone with Cale! Her emotions all over the place, with not a thing in her head with which to explain her Freudian slip, Anstey started to panic.

'I just have to go and tell somebody the good news,' Mrs Quartermaine beamed delightedly, and was half-way to the door. 'I'll go and see Netty.'

Anstey was on her feet as the door closed behind her. She had nearly reached the door herself when, without her so much as having heard Cale move, his hand on her arm halted her.

Her heart threatening to jump out of her body, Anstey could still find nothing to say to him. Forced to cease her flight, she felt him turn her inexorably to face him.

'You don't think that there's a little something we should discuss?' he queried mildly.

She cast him a quick look and pulled out of his hold. But with her insides belonging to anyone but her, all she could find to utter was, 'I ... I'm sorry. I didn't mean ...' She faltered, and when Cale had nothing to say, but waited for her to go on, his very waiting silence seemed to compel her to go on. And suddenly, she was gabbling the explanation, 'I know you're quite capable of defending yourself, but since—well, I know you have your own reasons for not wanting your mother to know that Rosie is Lester's daughter—until you think the time is right to tell her. But—but, when you were in the hot-seat just now, I knew that you were defending my right to be Rosie's guardian.

It—just didn't seem—er—fair that I should sit there and—say nothing. But,' she raced on, 'I didn't mean to ...' Abruptly, she came to a full stop.

'You were defending me?' Cale queried, and smiled as he murmured, 'I find that somewhat encouraging.'

What he found encouraging was a little obscure to Anstey, but in her present state of confusion, she realised that that was no more than was to be expected.

'I'm sorry,' she said again, 'but with your mother—er—taking you to task, I—er ...'

'You thought you'd help me out?' he suggested.

'I don't think I was thinking at all,' she confessed.

Again he smiled, and there was even a touch of humour about him when, his tone mild still, he remarked, 'Well, my beautiful champion, in the words of the immortal bard—you've done it now.'

At one time Anstey thought she would have known if Shakespeare had ever written those words. But she wasn't thinking very clearly *before* Cale had called her 'my beautiful champion'; afterwards, she could only query, 'I'm not sure that I know what you mean?'

'You've seen my mother in action,' Cale replied. 'She puts a terrier to shame when she gets her teeth into anything. What you've done in your attempt to ease the situation for me,' he went on to inform her, 'is to ensure that neither of us gets any peace until we take that little trip up the aisle.'

'Y-you're—joking?' Anstey said faintly, but another flicked glance to his expression showed her that his smile had gone and that he was deadly serious.

'I'm not joking,' he replied, and, making her heart race, added, 'Neither was the suggestion I made that you marry me a joke.' Anstey's eyes were wide when he went on evenly, 'In all seriousness, Anstey, I think the best thing we can do all round is to marry.'

'Oh,' she said, and her heart beat a wild rhythm when she thought she saw a warm look in his eyes for her. Did Cale want to marry her because he felt something for her?

'You must see, as I do, that it's the only sensible way out of this mess.' Cale, with the logic she so hated, soon poured cold water on her highest hopes.

'Because,' she said slowly, striving hard to think with her head, 'because, if you marry me, your mother will bury her bone and—and won't give you any more hassle, and . . .'

'And you,' Cale took up, 'a Quartermaine, will be ensured a right to be consulted over the infant.' Anstey shook her head, but more from the fact that, mess though it certainly was, none of it seemed right. 'It's the only way, Anstey, believe me,' Cale resumed. 'In my view it's you who've been dealt the worst hand in all of this, and . . .' she looked at him as he paused, and was charmed by the trace of a smile that appeared on the corners of his mouth—and charmed by *him*, when he continued, 'while I'm aware that you must be under the constant strain of anxiety, I confess, I've grown to—like you well enough to want to relieve you of some of that anxiety.'

The way her heart leapt to hear him declare that he liked her made it no wonder to Anstey that she murmured, 'Thank you,' without being sure what she was thanking him for. With an effort, she found a wisp of control. A moment later, she was trying with all she had to think as logically as he always did. 'But,' she said when she thought she had got some of it together, 'supposing—supposing Joanna stays away a longish time and . . . and supposing you and I—er—do get married, won't your mother think it odd, to say the least, when we leave Rosie here for her and Netty to look after?'

He shrugged, but had a logical answer for that too. 'From what my mother said at dinner, she has accepted that a wife and mother might also want to keep her career. While you've told her of your dedication to your career, she also knows that my flat is an unsuitable place to rear a baby,' and while Anstey was hoping that Mrs Quartermaine never saw her 'mouse-hole' of a flat, Cale went on, 'My dear mother, I promise you, would be outraged if we did anything other than leave the infant here while we searched round the country areas for a suitable family home.'

'I see,' Anstey murmured, and thought she did see some light as she followed on, 'By which time—that is—before we have found that suitable family home, Joanna is sure to be back.'

'You're in front of me,' Cale remarked, as though her way of thinking out logic was hard to follow.

Anstey did her best to explain it more clearly. 'Joanna told me on the phone that it might take a year for her to think Lester out of her system. I thought she was joking, and I'm still fairly certain that she'll come home long before that. But if, in the meantime, you and I have got married, you'll be able to "delay" finding that home until you've found the right moment to tell your mother the truth about Rosie's parentage. By then,' she went on, 'Joanna is bound to be back and, with all this mess cleared up, you and I can be divorced.'

Anstey thought she had done a good job with her explanation. But the dark frown that came to Cale's face as she finished speaking made her brow wrinkle too as she tried to think up a better way to sum up her conclusions.

Cale, though, had a smart brain, and she realised that he must have caught the essence of what she was trying to say, when his frown gave way to a better-humoured look.

'Don't look so worried,' he teased. 'You're only getting married, not getting your head chopped off!' And as it started to dawn on Anstey that she must, without properly realising it, have agreed to marry him, he touched her arm

and turned her towards the door, telling her, 'I'm
endeavouring to relieve you of your anxieties, not to add to
them.'

They reached the door, but when he pulled it open and
she went to go through, Cale retained his hold on her arm.
She looked up in semi-enquiry, and her heart did another
merry dance because there was definitely a warm look in
his eyes this time, when he instructed softly, 'Don't worry.
Just leave everything to me.'

'I . . .' she said, without knowing what she wanted to say.
Then she didn't have the chance to say anything, because
Cale, as if he liked the look of her slightly parted lips, bent
his head.

Gently, he kissed her. 'Goodnight, my dear,' he said. In a
dream world, Anstey went to bed.

She awoke to be plagued by a nightmare of unease. Had
she truly agreed to marry Cale? Wide awake on the instant,
she could no more remember that morning than the night
before when, or if, she had ever told Cale that she would
marry him.

She could clearly remember all the logical reasons there
were for a marriage between the two of them to take place.
And could also remember how she had told Cale that when
all this mess was cleared up they could be divorced. But she
could not remember when she had actually said that she
would marry him, as he seemed to think she had. Suddenly,
it seemed all wrong. She wanted to marry him. Dearly did
she want to marry him. But she wanted to marry him from
love, not from logic, and certainly not because, to his
logical-thinking mind, it was expedient all round for them
to marry.

There was no gainsaying that it was expedient, though.
Cale was after a reconciliation between his mother and
Lester, and somehow Anstey had an idea that Cale always
got what he went after. She couldn't see it ever occurring to

him to balk at any hurdle that lay in his path once he had set his mind to something. Even if in this case it meant he would have to give up his much valued bachelorhood—be it only temporarily—he would do it. Things had gone badly awry when his mother had been outraged that her granddaughter was illegitimate. He'd had to decide then to bide his time to tell her that Rosie was Lester's offspring. But, having come this far, Cale would take it in his stride that he was going to have to tie himself up with someone he did not love.

Anstey pushed away her emotion that Cale did not love her, and looked for pluses. She found one in the fact that, while he was biding his time, he was also assuring that she had a right to be heard over Rosie—and for another plus, Cale had grown to like her.

After first looking in on the nursery, Anstey went down to breakfast. She found that Mrs Quartermaine was there alone, *and* at her most charming.

'Good morning, Anstey,' she greeted her with a warm smile. 'I'm afraid it's just the two of us. Your fiancé,' she went on as Anstey took her place at the table, 'is rather busy this morning.'

Oh, grief, Anstey thought, Mrs Quartermaine's determination to remind her that she was engaged to her son making her unsure if she was glad or sorry that Cale was not at breakfast with them. But as his mother graciously helped her to coffee and toast, and made a pleasant remark about the weather, Anstey suspected that he had been sent to give the builder another blasting on his parent's behalf.

'We didn't have much chance for a chat last night,' Mrs Quartermaine remarked, the subject of the fine spell of weather they were having out of the way. 'But, even though you must know how pleased it makes me that you and Cale have decided to do the decent thing where Rosie is concerned, I just wanted you to know also that I couldn't be more pleased that you are the girl whom Cale has chosen.'

Oh, lord! Anstey wished she hadn't come down to breakfast! Mrs Quartermaine looked so sincere, and she was being so nice to her, that it just was not the moment to reveal that she'd been more forced on Cale than selected.

'You're—pleased?' she murmured, realising that she was expected to say something.

'I couldn't be more so,' Mrs Quartermaine smiled. 'Forgive me, my dear,' she went on, 'but you no doubt know that Cale had many lady-friends before he met you. I'm just so pleased that he has chosen you rather than one of those hoity-toity types he used to—er—nightclub with.'

For 'hoity-toity', Anstey read 'sophisticated', and accepted that she was neither hoity-toity nor sophisticated, though for a moment, if that was the type Cale admired, she wished that she was both. But again Mrs Quartermaine was waiting for some reply, and as jealousy pierced her and she wished Mrs Quartermaine had left her in the dark about Cale's lady-friends, all Anstey could do was search to find some comment that might close the subject.

'It's the quiet ones that men like Cale have to watch out for,' she said, with her best attempt at a smile. To her surprise, Mrs Quartermaine not only returned her smile but, as if she had found the comment amusing, she laughed as she replied,

'I can see that my son will have to keep on his toes when you're married!'

The pattern of Anstey's morning followed the same pattern as the previous morning. After leaving the breakfast-room, she went to the nursery and did what she could to help Netty, then when Rosie was ready for an airing, she took her out in the solid but streamlined pram.

Many thoughts flitted through Anstey's mind on that walk, although thoughts of Cale predominated. Again she wished that his mother had not mentioned his lady-friends.

When jealousy at one stage became almost more than she could bear, she had a private battle where mutiny formed an opposition. For all of two minutes then, she was all for charging back to the house to announce that there was not going to be any wedding. That was until she remembered that, if Cale was still arguing the toss with the builder, her announcement would have to be made to Mrs Quartermaine. Anstey sighed, and was fed up again. It was only because Mrs Quartermaine had gone on and on, refusing to give the subject any rest, that she had got 'engaged' to her son in the first place. They'd never hear the end of it, if either one of them dared to tell her that they'd changed their minds, and that the engagement was off.

Reluctant to go back, Anstey stayed out with Rosie until she had just enough time to deliver her to Netty and tidy herself up before lunch. Even so she was a few minutes late when she hurried to the dining-room.

Whether Cale had been on his way to come looking for her she didn't know. But as she opened the dining-room door, she found him standing there in front of her. And suddenly as she looked up at him and he halted to stand looking down at her, everything faded from Anstey's mind, and she was aware of nothing but him.

She thought there was a gentle look in the grey eyes that scrutinised her upturned face, and all at once her heart began to pound. She gave no thought to what was in her eyes, and could only remember that he had been gentle too when last night he had kissed her and had told her to leave everything to him.

Her throat went dry, and as she stared up at him, she felt near to fainting from the thought that she was engaged to marry this tall, dear, clever man . . .

Cale's eyes were continuing to hold hers warm and steady, when Anstey saw a smile start to break on his mouth. He stretched out a hand to her and, suddenly, she was trembling.

Just as suddenly, great clamouring alarm bells went off in her head, and Anstey was in fear and panic that Cale might have read in her eyes that which she must keep hidden. At all costs he must not know that she was in love with him! Oh, dear heaven, had she given herself away?

'Had a good morning?' she heard some actress buried deep within her chirrup brightly, vaguely recalling that they were words which he had once said to her. She sidestepped him and his hand fell to his side.

Afterwards she realised that she had only read warmth in his expression, gentleness in his eyes, because that was what she wanted to read. Later she realised that Cale's movement to reach out for her had not been the involuntary one she had imagined, but had been purely a movement to usher her further into the room.

She took another few steps across the carpet, but she was still battling to get herself together when she saw Mrs Quartermaine, and stopped dead. It was not just seeing her hostess that caused her to halt in her tracks, however, but the fact that Mrs Quartermaine had other company!

Anstey had already started to feel vibes of suspicion when Mrs Quartermaine, with a pleasant smile, remarked, 'You remember Mr Midwinter, Anstey?'

'Yes, of course,' she replied, and went to shake hands with him.

Her vibes were still active when the four of them sat down at the luncheon table. The last time she had sat at a meal table with the minister, Anstey recalled, she had assumed he had been there because of some longstanding invitation. But, if not very much older now, she reckoned that she was a great deal wiser.

It soon became apparent that the vicar was not at the table from some longstanding arrangement this time either.

Just as it became apparent to Anstey that her notion that
Cale had been on some errand in connection with his
mother's running battle with her builder had been way off
the mark. Cale, it seemed, had been to the vicarage to catch
the minister in between services, where he had discussed a
few matters and, at the same time, had invited him to lunch.

The first Anstey heard of any of the matters discussed
was when Mrs Quartermaine, while partaking elegantly of
her soup, enquired, 'Your parents won't be upset that
you're to be married from our local church, Anstey?'

Struck dumb, Anstey did her best to keep her composure.
'Er—no, I don't think so,' she murmured, belatedly
realising that she hadn't given her parents a thought when
she had considered marrying, and being divorced from,
Cale. Nor did she have time to give them much thought
then, for Mrs Quartermaine was going on.

'If you explain to them that, traditionally, all Quartermaine brides are married from Quiet Ways at St James's,
I'm sure they'll understand.' Anstey was still taking that in
when Mrs Quartermaine, a born organiser, turned to her
son. 'You'll have to stay the night at The Carpenter's Arms,
Cale, as your father did before you. That is,' she smiled,
'unless you intend to drive down from London on Friday
morning. You certainly can't stay Thursday night in the
same house as . . .'

'Friday!' Anstey's head was whirling. Surely they
weren't talking in terms of her and Cale getting married
this Friday! Her eyes flew to him, but it was the vicar who
answered.

'We're arranging for a special licence. We have four
clear days—ample time,' he assured her cheerfully.

Still Anstey could not take it in. 'You . . . We . . .' She
flicked another glance to Cale, but he seemed to be enjoying
his soup too well to want to give her a hand. 'You're
arranging the wedding for *this* Friday?' she asked the vicar,

needing confirmation of what appeared to be all cut and dried.

'Friday isn't convenient?' Mrs Quartermaine cut in a little stiffly, causing Anstey to turn her head in her direction.

Oh, crumbs, Anstey thought, on seeing that frost warnings were imminent. 'It's—a trifle soon, don't you think?' she asked lamely.

'As a matter of fact, I don't. In my opinion,' Mrs Quartermaine told her, 'the marriage ceremony should have been performed long before this. A year ago, to be candid.'

Anstey had never known Mrs Quartermaine anything other than candid. 'Yes—but . . .' she began, but suddenly she realised that, given that the circumstances were what everyone supposed them to be, she just hadn't anything to argue with. 'I'll—have to arrange to have Friday off,' she agreed faintly.

'Now,' said Mrs Quartermaine, that hiccup dealt with, soon re-donning her organising hat, 'I propose a small wedding reception. Small, for obvious reasons. Naturally,' she was smiling again, 'you'll want your family here, Anstey. Then there's . . .'

Anstey, realising that she could not ask her parents to come and see her married, blanked off to what else Mrs Quartermaine was saying. For one thing, once her mother was over the shock of learning that her only daughter was to be married—*this coming Friday*—and to a man she had never heard her mention, much less met, she would go all dewy-eyed. And, with a divorce pending, that just wasn't fair. Anstey knew she would definitely not be inviting her parents when she realised that, if Rosie was not actually there at the church, then she would certainly be brought down for the proud grandparents to coo over at the reception. As she had told Cale, her visits back to her old home were frequent enough for her mother to have noticed that her slender proportions had remained constant during the last four years.

Anstey was in the throes of hearing her mother vehemently disclaiming to Mrs Quartermaine, 'I don't know who that baby belongs to, but she *certainly* wasn't born to *my* daughter,' when she became aware that Mrs Quartermaine had just asked her a question.

'I'm sorry, I didn't . . .' she began, and discovered that, despite their soup plates having been exchanged for the main course some time since, Cale was not so involved with food that he had not kept an ear tuned to the conversation.

'If you'd like any of your family to stay overnight with you on Thursday, my mother will be pleased to have rooms made ready for them at Quiet Ways,' he relayed the substance of Mrs Quartermaine's question.

'Thank you,' Anstey muttered, but, feeling suddenly frustrated in the situation about which she was stifled to do anything, she could not see why he shouldn't do a bit of wriggling for a change. 'But,' she fixed him with an impotent glare, 'you know why I can't ask my parents to be here.'

His answer to her glare was to smile. 'Of course, darling,' he said smoothly. 'Forgive me for forgetting.' Without turning a hair, he extended his smile to his mother. 'Anstey's parents are abroad at the moment,' he lied handsomely, 'and won't be back for some time.'

'Well, we certainly can't wait for them to return,' said Mrs Quartermaine, who liked to have her priorities in order. And with a placatory smile to Anstey, 'We'll delay Rosie's christening until they get back to make it up to them.'

With a vision of fresh complications looming if the next bee Mrs Quartermaine got into her bonnet was her granddaughter's christening, Anstey opted out. She reckoned she had enough to cope with without having to perjure her soul by declaring in church that she was Rosie's mother.

Lunch eventually came to an end, a satisfactory end as far as Mrs Quartermaine was concerned, judging by the smile on her face. At least she's got something to think about other than her younger son, Anstey thought dismally. Then discovered, as Mrs Quartermaine took the vicar off to show him her roses, that she had been left alone with Cale.

'Whose idea was Friday?' she asked as she folded her napkin.

Cale studied her solemn face for a brief moment, before he told her evenly, 'The sooner we're married, the sooner your rights over the little one will be established.'

Anstey realised then that whether they got married this Friday or a month from now, she had no quibble—other than that in a month from now, Joanna might be home. Though the way Joanna was taking her time . . . Oh, what was the use? The speed at which Cale worked, he'd probably have them divorced a week after Joanna did come back. That thought, though, prompted her to ask another question.

'Do we have to get married in St James's? I know,' she went on quickly, when his right eyebrow lifted in enquiry, 'that it's traditional in your family. But, since we plan to be divorced as soon as we can, wouldn't it be better if we married in a register office?'

She realised that Cale was giving her question full consideration when, his look thoughtful, it was some seconds before he spoke. Then, ready to grant her smallest wish, it seemed, he replied, 'If a register office is what you want, I can certainly change the arrangements.' He paused, and looked so as if he was about to say something—though at the same time as if it was something he didn't want to say—that Anstey, fearing that she wasn't going to like it, whatever it was, just had to ask,

'You've—thought of a snag?'

'Hmm,' he hesitated, 'I was just wondering—which one of us is going to tell my mother that, instead of St James's, we've decided on a register office wedding—and, incidentally, that we intend to break the Quartermaine tradition?'

'Oh, lord,' Anstey groaned, having enough to endure without inviting more. 'Leave it,' she said wearily, and got up from her chair. 'Leave things as they are. I'll marry you in St James's.'

She was at the door, and had it open, when she realised just how confused she must be. For she could have sworn that Cale was sounding exceedingly pleased with himself, when she caught his murmured, 'Certainly, my dear.'

CHAPTER NINE

WHEN later that afternoon they began the drive back to London, Anstey had come to terms with what she couldn't fight. She believed, too, that she was clear of the confusion which had beset her at lunch time.

They had been motoring only some short while, however, when doubt returned. So far the journey had been spent with Cale making affable conversation, or in companionable silence. Either way, he was at his most agreeable. Given the fact that this coming Friday he was going to have to relinquish his much-prized bachelor-hood—be it only for a short while—all at once Anstey considered that he was being *too* agreeable.

Suddenly she was recalling how pleased she had thought he'd sounded when as she left him after lunch he'd murmured, 'Certainly, my dear'. Just as if, having got what he wanted, he would agree to anything she suggested!

Her heart gave a sudden flip at the thought that it was as though he wanted to marry her, and could not wait for Friday! Her heartbeat steadied to a dejected thud as she recognised that thought as pure wishful thinking. But a niggle of suspicion started when, whichever way she looked at it, she realised that he did not seem as averse to the idea of giving up his freedom as she would have supposed.

Her suspicions aroused, she just had to question—why? She knew him for a devious devil—but had she again walked into his parlour without knowing it?

Anstey set her mind to remembering how his marriage proposal had come about. Cale, she recalled without effort, had only suggested she marry him in the first place because of the relentless pressure his mother had kept up in her efforts to get him to see where his duty lay.

And she had swallowed it! Cale was *used* to pressure! No man could head a firm the way he did without being capable of daily working under constant pressure. Was it likely that a man who could cope as he had to in business without folding would fold and give in, purely because his mother telephoned to have a daily nag?

'You don't have a car, Anstey?' Cale interrupted her thoughts to enquire pleasantly.

'I don't drive,' she replied shortly, too shaken by her realisation to want to be polite.

Cale turned his head to glance at her sharply, but if he had noted her tone, he remained pleasant when he went on to inform her, 'I'll have a few loose ends to clear up on Thursday, so, if it's all right with you, I'll get one of the company's drivers to take you down to Quiet Ways that evening.'

'Talking of loose ends,' Anstey jumped in bluntly, needing a few straight answers, 'why, would you mind telling me honestly, do you want to marry me?'

She was looking at him, but his eyes were on the road ahead and she could tell nothing of what he was thinking from his profile. When it looked, though, as if she might have to wait for ever for an answer, he flicked her a glance, and said slowly, 'I—thought you knew.'

'So did I,' Anstey said shortly. 'It's taken until now for it to dawn on me that you're so used to being under pressure in your work that you could more than handle any pressure your mother applied—with both hands tied behind your back.'

'Ah,' said Cale.

That wasn't sufficient for Anstey. 'What exactly does "Ah" mean?' she wanted to know.

Again Cale did not immediately reply, but when he did,

she was to wish that she had never started that particular ball rolling.

'I didn't tell you before—not because I underrated your intelligence, but because it didn't seem necessary to tell you,' he began, his words slow still, as if he was determined to be as honest as she had asked, and did not wish to leave anything out. 'I'm not certain that it has any relevance now,' he continued, 'but rather than have you think I've been dishonest with you, I'll tell you that it would suit me quite well to be able to state that I'm a newly married man.'

For some seconds his reply left her as much in the dark as she had been before. Her first notion was that there must be some business reason why he should want to state that he was a newly married man. She scrapped the idea. His name was too respected for him to be anything other than as straight as a die in his business life. His personal life, then?

Suddenly Anstey remembered something his mother had said only that morning, and as jealousy bit, she couldn't think beyond some beautiful, hoity-toity and sophisticated lady-friend, when she asked, 'You're having—lady-friend—trouble, at the moment?' She waited, hoping with all she had that he would deny it.

'And *how*,' he answered. 'Though to be more accurate,' he admitted, 'the lady's husband is proving the greater problem.'

'She's married!' Feeling sick inside, Anstey looked away. She guessed his reply must have been a nod of his head, for he did not answer verbally.

Silence reigned in the car, and she realised he had said all he intended to on the subject. For her part, she didn't want to know any more. She felt quite ill at the knowledge that Cale had a more prime motive for marrying her than she had thought. That prime motive: to continue what must be a very heady illicit love-affair. The main reason Cale was marrying her was in order to be able to tell any enraged husband who came banging on his door that he was hardly likely to be interested in another's wife, when he had a brand new wife of his own.

Anstey very nearly told Cale right then that he needn't bother to send a chauffeur to collect her on Thursday, because she had no intention of marrying him on Friday. Just in time, though, she realised that their other reasons for being married still stood. Despite Cale's revelations, nothing had changed. That being so, Anstey went hot at the thought that if she went ahead and told him that the wedding was off, he would know straight away that her only reason for withdrawing was because of what he had just told her. It wouldn't take him a minute to come to the conclusion that even her rights regarding little Rosie counted for nothing against the emotions she felt for him.

Jealousy was still picking at Anstey when she discovered a need to know just how deeply he was involved with the woman he was prepared to go to such lengths for. Was she a 'special' one, or was she just one of a long line?

'You—er—normally go in for—um—dating married women?' she asked. Cale did not answer. 'I mean,' darts of jealousy pushed her on, 'have you had many women-friends—m-many affairs?'

Realising when he did not reply that he had taken exception to her line of enquiry, Anstey started to regret her probing. Suddenly though, he turned his head, and she saw that there was even a faint look of a smile on his mouth when he uttered, 'I've been around a few years, Anstey. Had I wanted a celibate life, I'd have joined a monastery.'

'I suppose you would,' she had to agree, only to be startled when Cale, obviously seeing no reason not to question in kind—since she had started it—enquired, a shade sharply,

'How about you—have there been many lovers?'

Anstey still did not know if his current lady-friend was

'special' to him. But, taken aback to have her question up-ended and returned, she concentrated on making her voice uncaring so he should know that nothing of what he had revealed bothered her in the slightest.

'One lives in hopes, of course,' she told him blithely, 'but, given the odd close call, so far, I'm still a virgin.'

'You're a . . .!' Cale left that exclamation in mid-air. 'Ye gods!' he breathed as if winded. Then his tone underwent a dramatic change and was the severest she had yet heard, when he went on to say sternly, 'Remind me, Anastasia Eldridge, to tell you a few facts of life some time.'

She guessed he was referring to that night when she had wanted him, as he had wanted her. On reflection, she supposed that not many men would have shown the self-control he had—furious though he had been with her at the time. Only then did she realise that she could have found herself in difficulties if, passion still about him, he had refused to take no for an answer.

'That,' she told him stiffly, 'won't be necessary,' and looked out of the side window.

For the remainder of the journey, she was eaten up with jealousy. Was it that Cale had so much self-control; or was it that, in the middle of a steamy love-affair with a married woman, anything Anastasia Eldridge had sparked in him was insignificant beside his lady-love's charms?

They were nearing her flat and she was not liking Cale very much, when, with the cheek of the devil, in her opinion, he suggested suavely, 'We'd better make arrange-ments for you to move your things into my place. I can . . .'

'Good grief!' she erupted, denouncing her contrary heart as no friend as it started to beat excitedly at the very thought. 'There's no need for us to live together, surely! In any case,' she went on swiftly, terrified that she might give in to an inner yearning to do just that, 'our marriage will be over in five minutes, so it's hardly worth the bother of my packing my belongings and moving into your spare room, only to have to move them back when—when—all this mess is straightened out.'

She had thought she had sounded convincing, and although she noticed that Cale didn't look exactly ecstatic to have his wishes opposed, he must have thought there was something in what she said, for he did not argue the point.

'It occurred to me that my mother might take it into her head to come and pay us a visit,' was all he said. 'However, I'm sure I'll be able to think of something, should that situation arise.'

'I'm sure you will.' Anstey didn't doubt it.

'Though, for the look of the thing, but only if you're in agreement, of course,' he went on blandly, 'I do think that perhaps we'd better plan to go off somewhere together after the wedding ceremony.'

Anstey's heart let her down badly. Her head said that the idea, if logical, was unthinkable. Her heart betrayed her. 'So long as I'm back for work on Monday,' she conceded.

'Your—career—will be to the forefront of my mind,' Cale told her solemnly.

Perversely, Anstey just had to laugh. Though even as she laughed, she was telling him, 'Cut the sarcasm, Quartermaine.' Cale, as if he liked her laugh, grinned.

She was not laughing when at the door of her flat Cale turned the key she had just given him, and handed it back to her. If he says goodbye with something like 'See you in church' I'll hit him, she thought.

He did not say anything of the kind, but stood for a moment looking into her eyes. Then, to make her pulses race, he drew her right hand up to his lips and pressed a light kiss to the back of it. 'It'll be all right, Anstey,' he told her softly. 'Don't worry,' he added, and was gone.

Anstey did worry. What she was about to do hadn't seemed so bad when he had been with her, but alone in her flat she had too much time to think.

She went to work on Monday and, as she had expected, found Mr Sallis uncooperative when she asked him for Friday off. Anstey came the nearest she had ever come that day to telling him what he could do with his job. She owned that her temper was burning on a short fuse just lately.

'If you must, you must,' he eventually acceded to her request, when she stubbornly insisted. 'But I shall be very glad when you have your domestic problems sorted out.'

So shall I, she thought, disgruntled, and went home that night with a whole evening stretching before her with nothing to do but think.

At seven o'clock, her phone rang. Feeling pangs of guilt that the caller might be her mother, Anstey went to answer it. No sooner had she picked it up than her emotions went haywire. It was Cale.

'Have dinner with me?' he asked.

The words to accept his invitation flew to her lips. Jealousy denied them. 'I've just had something to eat,' she lied, all of a sudden damned if she'd be a substitute if Mondays were the only evenings his lady-love couldn't see him.

'You sound—uptight?' Cale probed.

'That's probably because I am,' she snapped, and slammed down the phone, to immediately regret her action.

She realised that she must be in a fine state when she spent the next ten minutes first in thinking that if she'd stayed talking to Cale he might have made everything sound perfectly reasonable, then in being glad that she had slammed the phone down. What she didn't need was to have more of his logic pushed down her throat. He'd had all day to call her, anyway, she fumed. What did he think she was that he could only remember her when he realised that he had no dinner companion for the evening?

Anstey spent most of the evening loving Cale and railing against him. She finally took herself off to bed resenting him, his logic, his deviousness, and even the fact that he had not insisted that she move in with him. Her jealousy peaking, she was certain then that the only reason he had not insisted was because he'd had an afterthought and had realised that to have her in residence was likely to cramp his style. For, whatever else he was, Anstey just could not credit that he would bring his lady-love to his flat—not while his wife lived there.

She awoke on Tuesday morning, more rebellious than uptight. Rebellion stayed with her the whole of that morning, and was her companion when she went out for a breath of air at lunch time. She had given little thought to what she was going to wear to be married in, but she was just passing a bridal gown shop window, when she suddenly halted mid-step. There, just asking to be purchased, was the most gorgeous mid-calf-length, if unfussy, wedding dress.

A lump came into her throat, and her rebellion dipped for a few seconds. A dreamy look came into her eyes, and suddenly all she could see was Cale turning and waiting for her as she floated down the aisle dressed in the model on display.

The picture vanished when she became aware of a prickling sensation at the backs of her eyes. Horrified, she thought for one awful moment that she was going to break down and cry in the middle of the shopping centre.

Anstey gained control of her emotions when it suddenly dawned on her that she couldn't have the dress anyway. The dress was white, and while any other colour would be all right by Mrs Quartermaine, white, Anstey recalled, was definitely out. So she thought until her spirit of rebellion suddenly re-awoke. Dammit, she was entitled. She marched into the shop. Fifteen minutes later she came out again— laden with a large paper carrier.

Feelings of rebellion stayed with her right up until the time she returned to her flat and went to put her lunch-time purchase on a hanger. Suddenly then, as she stared at her lovely dress, she just knew that she couldn't go through with it. Had Cale loved her . . .

Anstey dragged her thoughts away from what could never be, and tried to remember where she had put the card Cale had once given her which bore his home telephone number. She calculated that the switchboard at Quartermaine Holdings would be closed now, but he had to be told, and the sooner, the better.

At ten past midnight she climbed into bed having spent a frustrated evening dialling Cale's home number in vain. Cale, no doubt painting the town red somewhere with his mistress, was not in.

Anstey did not sleep well that night, nor did she sleep well the following night. Nor had she been able to contact Cale. If he was being deliberately elusive, he couldn't have done better! When she rang his office, he was at a meeting. When she rang his home, there was no reply.

When she left her bed on Thursday morning, Anstey had a feeling that it was too late now to do anything about it. By now Mrs Quartermaine, with her organising ability, would have the small wedding reception sorted out, and Cale and the vicar would have the special licence organised. In accepting that, Anstey suddenly realised that she was not now feeling as bad about marrying Cale as she had.

Whether her love for him was at the back of her more settled feeling or whether that feeling stemmed from the indisputable knowledge that if she didn't marry him even her right to visit Rosie might well vanish, Anstey did not know. What she did know, as she made her way to Elton Diesel, was that she was not going to attempt to contact him that day.

She had been at her desk for no more than half an hour,

though, when her more settled feelings were suddenly sent flying. Why hadn't Cale tried to contact her? True she had slammed the phone down on him the last time he had made contact, but even so . . .

Anstey spent the rest of the day on the fidget. Cale had said he'd send a car to take her down to Quiet Ways that evening. The least he could have done was to ring and tell her at what time to expect his driver. That was, unless Cale had changed his mind about giving up his freedom, and had decided not to send a driver at all!

Too proud to ring Cale to find out, Anstey left Elton Diesel that night having worked herself up into a fine state. If Cale Quartermaine hadn't got the decency to ring her, she fumed as she turned into her street, well . . . Suddenly her eyes widened and all thoughts ceased. There, outside where she lived, stood the most fantastic, luxurious Rolls-Royce!

It couldn't be! Or was it? With no wish to make a fool of herself by marching up to the uniformed chauffeur, Anstey donned the air of someone who hadn't seen him, and approached her front door.

She had no sooner turned her back to go through the door, however, when a stocky middle-aged man, more nimble than he looked, was out of the car and was respectfully addressing her back.

'Excuse me, madam.' Anstey turned. 'May I ask if you are Miss Eldridge?' he enquired.

'Mr Quartermaine sent you?' she enquired in return, and smiled her first natural smile of the day.

An hour later, feeling like royalty, Anstey was in the back of the Rolls-Royce and was on her way to Quiet Ways. Ted, her driver, was the ultimate in courtesy, she had discovered. 'No, thank you, madam,' had been his reply when, nowhere near ready, she had asked him if he'd like to come up for a cup of tea while he waited.

'I may be some time,' she had thought she'd better mention.

'Whatever you say, Miss Eldridge,' he had answered, unperturbed.

'You don't mind waiting?'

'My instructions were to attend to your every wish.'

Anstey had left him, and hurried round her flat packing a case in haste, and wishing she had thought to ask Cale—since his logic decreed that they go off somewhere together after the reception—where they were going.

'Thank you, Ted,' she said, when at Quiet Ways his nimble-footedness startled her again, for he was out of the Rolls and holding the passenger door open before she had more than moved to the edge of her seat.

'My pleasure, Miss Eldridge,' he replied politely, but shook her somewhat when, as he extracted her luggage from the boot, he added, 'I shall be on duty to take you to church in the morning, after I've driven the rest of the wedding party to church.'

'You're coming down from London especially?' she queried, hiding her surprise. Except for some poor cuckold husband, of course, she would have thought Cale unlikely to tell anyone else that he was to be married.

'I'm staying overnight at The Carpenter's Arms,' Ted replied. 'Mr Quartermaine booked me in when he made his own reservation.'

'Of course,' Anstey smiled, becoming more adept at hiding her surprise with each new disclosure. 'I'll take these,' she said, when Ted would have carried her case and her paper carrier into the house. 'Goodbye,' she bade him. She crossed a strip of gravel to realise that learning Cale would be near to Quiet Ways that night had made her feel much less churned up inside than she had done.

'Anstey!' Mrs Quartermaine, a suddenly warm and smiling Mrs Quartermaine, had the front door open before

Anstey could put her case down to ring the doorbell. 'Come in, my dear, come in,' she invited.

Feeling much welcomed, Anstey deposited her luggage upstairs and, after looking in on a never-happier Netty and a positively blooming Rosie, she went downstairs to join Mrs Quartermaine for dinner.

As the evening progressed, she began to feel more and more wanted as a member of the family. Not that Mrs Quartermaine was gushing, that wasn't her way, but with sincere charm, she chatted all through dinner and had not run out of conversation pieces when they adjourned to the drawing-room.

Strangely, though, apart from an early reference to everything being ready for tomorrow, not once did she speak of the wedding again—or of Rosie either. Both subjects had caused friction in the past, Anstey mused, so perhaps Mrs Quartermaine was anxious to avoid any subject which might provoke a hint of discord on this, her wedding eve.

It was half past ten when, realising she had just spent a pleasant evening with her hostess, Anstey looked at her watch and made noises about going to bed.

'Would you like a nightcap, Anstey? Or some warm milk, or . . .'

'Nothing, thank you.' Anstey left her chair, but only to have her goodnight to Mrs Quartermaine interrupted when the phone in the room rang.

Mrs Quartermaine went to answer it, and Anstey was undecided whether she should leave the room without saying goodnight, which might seem churlish after the pleasant evening, or whether to wait and thereby intrude on a private conversation.

Her dilemma was resolved when Mrs Quartermaine turned and held the phone out to her. 'It's for you,' she smiled.

Cale was the only person, apart from the chauffeur, who knew where she was! Her heart immediately quickened its beat, and Anstey went forward and took hold of the phone.

'Hello,' she said, and had to endure a lengthy pause, before she suddenly heard Cale's deep and well remembered voice.

'Ted tells me he delivered you safely,' he remarked, and sounded so much as if her safe arrival mattered to him that Anstey forgot every bit of how on Tuesday and on Wednesday she had been ready to tell him that she would not marry him.

'If you've seen Ted,' she replied, realising that she was picking up nuances which just weren't there, 'you must have arrived at The Carpenter's Arms—er—safely too.'

'I've just checked in,' he replied, to cause her to think crazily that he'd got to a phone to ring her at the first opportunity.

Crazy wasn't the word for it, Anstey suddenly saw. Particularly was she being crazy when, since Monday, the phone in her flat had stayed dead.

'You've been working, no doubt,' she said sharply, and was instantly horrified. She had sounded just like some jealous shrew! Oh, grief, she quailed, as a year passed before Cale made any reply!

'You thought—I was out—having fun?' he queried slowly.

'Out having fun?' she asked in return, panicking and certain that he had recognised her jealousy for what it was. 'I'm not with you,' she lied. 'You said—er—the last time I saw you, that you'd have a few loose ends to clear up. I assumed you meant you'd be working late at your office. By the way,' she went on in a rush, 'is Ted driving you to the church tomorrow, too?' Oh, hell, she thought, realising that panic had left her with very little brain-power. 'Of course,' she answered her own question, 'I forgot, you've got your own car.'

'I have,' he replied, 'but,' and suddenly she could have sworn he was smiling, for there was definitely good humour in his voice, when he revealed, 'it's traditional for a Quartermaine to walk to church from The Carpenter's Arms on his wedding day.'

'A tradition you're going to uphold?'

'Can't let the side down,' he replied lightly.

'That would never do,' she said and, feeling suddenly weakened by him, she grew afraid that she might say something else without thinking first. 'I'm just going to bed,' she told him.

'Then—goodnight, sweet Anstey,' he said softly. Before she could find an answering 'Goodnight' the line went dead.

Friday dawned bright and sunny. Anstey realised it was too late to have second thoughts, or even third and fourth thoughts, when Mrs Quartermaine in person came smiling into her room with a breakfast tray.

'I ...' Anstey gasped, but as she guessed it must be another tradition for a Quartermaine bride to be brought breakfast in bed on her wedding day, 'Thank you,' she accepted.

'Thank you, Anstey,' Mrs Quartermaine replied, as she placed the bed tray over her knees. Anstey was still trying to work out what that sincere-sounding 'Thank you' meant when Mrs Quartermaine, as if she had a million and one things to do, went quickly from the room.

Any further puzzling over what that 'Thank you' meant went from Anstey's head as she wondered if she should hurry up and eat her breakfast so as to be able to go and give her hostess a hand.

She then remembered her future mother-in-law's organising ability, and had a fair idea that she might be more of a hindrance than a help if Mrs Quartermaine had to continually halt in what she was doing to tell her what she wanted done next.

Time dragged slowly until the time came for her to get into her white dress. Then it flew. Anstey had thought herself unflappable, but she discovered that in certain circumstances she was not. Her hair didn't look right, her make-up didn't look right, and worse, she began to think she had made a colossal mistake in the purchase of her white dress.

In truth, she was undergoing a severe attack of nerves. She tried to tell herself it was ridiculous. This marriage ceremony was a formality, for goodness' sake! The ink would barely be dry on the marriage certificate when she and Cale would be getting divorced. None of it was a help.

She finally had her blonde wavy hair looking the way it should, and her light covering of make-up about right, when, after a tap on her door, Mrs Quartermaine came in with a small but exquisitely arranged posy of red roses.

'Oh, Mrs Quartermaine!' Anstey exclaimed, and felt near to tears.

'Cale sent them,' Mrs Quartermaine told her, and without the least sign of disapproval at Anstey's white dress, she said, 'You look positively beautiful, my dear,' and looked near to tears herself before adding in a bracing tone, 'I shall have to go if I'm not to be late. Ted will be back for you in a few minutes.'

Anstey needed all her will-power not to cry after she had gone. 'Oh, Cale,' she whispered, emotion choking her as she looked at the roses he had sent.

It took several deep breaths before she decided that she felt on a more even keel. Taking the flowers with her, she left her room and descended the stairs. Ted was back a few minutes later, but by that time, she was a bundle of nerves again.

'Good morning, Miss Eldridge,' he smiled, clearly admiring the picture she made as he assisted her into the Rolls.

By the time they arrived at the village church, Anstey was clutching at her posy as if it was a life-line. She was met at the church door by Mr Midwinter, but although she saw him say something, she had no idea what it was.

Deaf to anything, she was blind too to the people on either side of the aisle as she walked with the vicar to where Cale, tall and immaculate, stood waiting for her. Then she was beside Cale, and he turned to look at her.

She thought he seemed slightly pale, and as tense as she felt, then her eyes found his. Steady grey eyes stayed on her. Agitatedly she knew again that her white dress was all wrong, then suddenly she realised from something in Cale's eyes that he was glad she had worn white. There was admiration there too, and a gentleness. Slowly then a trace of a smile appeared on his mouth, and all at once Anstey began to feel very much better. When Cale's smile made it, she smiled back at him, and faced then that she was marrying him because she wanted to marry him.

In love with him, she made her vows with love. As if there was no pretence in him either, Cale made his vows in a clear sincere voice. Briefly, Anstey was the happiest she had ever been. It did not last.

After signing the marriage register, they both received Mrs Quartermaine's warm congratulations, and Anstey left the vestry with her hand tucked into Cale's arm. She owned as they passed through the church door that her emotions were all out of gear. But as her eyes got used to the brilliant sunlight, and she espied a photographer setting up his tripod, so other shapes and sizes became more distinct, and Anstey's emotions became a confused mass.

At first she thought the crowd standing about were all villagers. But as her eyes adjusted to the strong light, suddenly she recognised one person whom she knew for a fact was not a local. Joanna . . .!

Too amazed to even begin to think, Anstey saw that Joanna, appearing to be in better health than she had ever seen her, and with a superb tan into the bargain, was standing with Rosie in her arms—right next to a tanned-looking Lester!

As if in slow motion, Anstey turned her head to Cale, wanting someone to explain for her all that her brain was too stunned to take in. But Cale was not looking at her. She saw that his eyes had followed hers, and noticed that the expression on his face as he stared at his brother was grim.

Her thought processes starting to re-awaken, Anstey looked for Mrs Quartermaine. She did not have to look far. For while the professional photographer was still adjusting his tripod, Mrs Quartermaine stood a photographic distance away from Joanna and Lester, and was busy with her own camera. The beaming smile on her face was there to reveal that whatever sins Lester had committed in the past, his mother had forgiven him everything.

'Give Rosie to Lester, Joanna dear,' her words echoed back to Anstey. 'While we're waiting, I'll take my first recorded picture of Lester holding his daughter.'

Reeling with the knowledge that Mrs Quartermaine knew the truth about Rosie, Anstey saw Joanna hand Rosie over and then step out of camera range. Shaken rigid as she was, only then did it start to dawn on Anstey that with the truth out, she had just married Cale when there had been absolutely no need! Shattered, she left Cale's side and moved towards Joanna without any real thought to what she was doing.

'Anstey . . .' she heard Cale call, but, guessing that he had heard what his mother had just said too, she kept on going.

'Anstey!' Joanna squealed, rushing to meet her half-way. 'You look fabulous, love. I couldn't resist coming to see you married,' she gabbled half apologetically. 'I know Cale expressly told Lester that we mustn't come, but . . .'

'Cale—did *what*!' Anstey exclaimed, her thinking power waking with a vengeance.

But Cale had followed her, and it was he who answered. 'Anstey, I . . .' he began, when Lester, with Rosie in his arms, came to interrupt,

'I know you specifically told me that Jo and I shouldn't dare to show our faces today, but . . .' He broke off as Cale turned on him.

Anstey caught a glimpse of Cale's expression, and realised that Lester was about to get it in the neck. But she was not staying around to listen. Mrs Quartermaine had come over to buttonhole both her sons when Anstey, more enraged than she had ever been in her life, took off at a sprint. Emotions in her which had been frayed ragged for most of the morning finally went haywire.

My God! she thought. No wonder Cale hadn't wanted Joanna and Lester to show their faces today. He knew damn well that if Joanna appeared before the wedding, the wedding would be off! He had *known* that his mother and Lester were reconciled! He had *known* that everything about Rosie was now out in the open! The cunning, conniving devil, he had needed a wife to act as cover while he continued his sordid affair with his married woman-friend. He had gone through the marriage ceremony, not for his mother's sake, Anstey raged as she espied the Rolls, nor to protect her rights to Rosie. Cale Quartermaine had married her for no one's sake but his own!

Anstey was never more glad that the chauffeur was so nimble on his feet. She supposed that he had ample experience of emergencies too, when he had the passenger door of the Rolls open as soon as he saw her sprinting towards it. Even if he, like the crowd she had to dodge through, didn't know what in creation was going on, his experience and training stood him in good stead.

'You were instructed to attend to my every wish,' Anstey reminded him in a rush. 'I wish to be taken to London as fast as you can get me there. It's traditional,' she told him for angry excuse.

The Rolls was on the move when Anstey saw Cale chasing near. She lowered the window and hurled his roses at him, and was heedless of his grim expression as the car outdistanced him.

In closing the window she caught a fleeting glimpse of the flabbergasted expressions of the people behind him. And that suited her just fine. Cale Quartermaine had made one hell of a fool out of her—it was about time someone left *him* looking foolish!

CHAPTER TEN

ANSTEY was still boiling when the Rolls stopped outside her flat. 'Thank you, Ted. You've made splendid time,' she told him as he assisted her to alight.

'With a vehicle like this, Mrs Quartermaine,' he told her unflappably, 'it took no effort.'

Her heart lurched at being addressed as Mrs Quartermaine, and she was suddenly too choked to find any words other than a mumbled, 'Goodbye.'

Any dent in her fury was soon overcome when in her flat she hurried to the bedroom and tore off her wedding dress. All her fury was directed at Cale as she hurled her lovely dress into a corner and pulled on cotton slacks and a T-shirt. Had *she* walked into his parlour—she had *married* the rat!

Not yet done with the many unpleasant names she found to revile him with, there was little room in her head to wonder where Joanna and Lester had sprung from. Anstey was certain though, as she played back the scene outside the church in her mind, that Mrs Quartermaine had known, *before today*, that she was not Rosie's mother!

It explained, of course, why she had avoided speaking of Rosie last night. She had been afraid that some unthought word might have her slipping up, revealing that she knew that Joanna was her granddaughter's mother.

It became a trifle obscure, though, why Mrs Quartermaine had avoided the subject of the wedding too. It was obvious that Cale had been in touch with her, but even if he had asked her to keep quiet or his intended bride would call the wedding off, that still did not explain why she had avoided that subject also.

Anstey gave it up, but she was certain as her anger welled again that whatever he had told his mother, it was for sure that he had not told her his true reason for wanting to be married. Well acquainted with Mrs Quartermaine's high moral standards, Anstey knew his mother would have a fit if Cale breathed a word to her about the affair he was having with a married woman. 'Fit' wouldn't cover Mrs Quartermaine's reaction if Cale had then proceeded to tell her that he only wanted to be married in order to continue with his adulterous affair.

Knowing that if she let her anger leave she was likely to give way to tears, Anstey fumed silently against Cale, and wondered how speedily she could get the ceremony anulled.

Acting while she was still angry enough not to care about any consequences in store for Cale, she was just looking through the Yellow Pages for a solicitor, when there was a knock on her door.

She was in no mood for a chat if Hazel, hearing her moving about, had decided to come up to while away half an hour. But, remembering Hazel's goodness to her in the past, Anstey laid down the trade telephone directory, and went to open the door. Promptly, her mouth fell agape.

In shock, she realised that Cale must not only have gone like the wind to get his car from The Carpenter's Arms, but that he must have driven like the devil to have got here so fast. She took a rocky step backwards, whereupon, not waiting to be invited in, Cale made her take another step backwards when he moved forward and closed the door. He was looking more casual than the determined light in his eyes decreed, when he asked evenly, 'What was all that about back at St James's?'

It was his nerve that did it. His cool utter nerve! Enraged by his cheek, and wishing she had thought when she had hurled his roses at him to hurl her wedding ring at him too, Anstey snatched the ring from her finger.

'Thanks for the loan,' she said icily, holding out the gold band, 'but . . .'

'You just put that back on!' Cale ordered sharply, his casual attitude soon gone.

'Like blazes I'll put it back on!' Anstey erupted. 'I may have promised to obey you—but that was only while the marriage lasted. It's over, Quartermaine,' she told him tartly. 'Had you arrived five minutes later, my solicitors would be in possession of my instructions.' She indicated the telephone book, and snapped, 'I was on the point of looking up the legal profession when you knocked on the door. Had I known . . .'

'Then I've saved you unnecessary trouble,' he cut in.

'Unnecessary?' she queried, not too taken with the sudden glint in his eyes.

'You're married to me, Anstey Quartermaine,' he told her toughly, 'and that's the way you'll stay.'

Was there no end to his nerve! Stunned by his utter gall, it took her a few moments to recover. 'You've just got to be joking!' she declared when she had her breath back. 'Aside from the fact that a divorce was all part of our marriage agreement . . .'

'When did I ever state that I was in agreement to our marriage ending in divorce?' Cale cut in crisply. And while Anstey stared, just not believing what she was hearing— that Cale had never intended that the marriage should be ended!—he was going on to confirm, 'I have no intention whatsoever, *wife*, of divorcing you, and for the record, no one, and that includes you, ever divorces a Quartermaine.'

Only just did Anstey stop her jaw dropping again. She surfaced to think that it was about time somebody told Cale Quartermaine that it wasn't his God-given right to declare what he would and would not do, and then to expect everyone to bow to his wishes.

'I've decided to set a new Quartermaine tradition,' she told him acidly.

'You already have,' he returned bluntly. 'There's nothing recorded to show that any other Quartermaine's bride lit out without stopping to have her photograph taken.'

'You think I should have stayed around—and smiled nicely for the cameraman—when I'd just found out what a double-dyed hound you really are?' Anstey flared, incensed, and was all geared to to say more, when Cale butted in,

'I know you're upset, and I'll concede you have some cause to be upset, but . . .'

'Big of you!' she tossed in.

'But,' he went on, 'I did, and do, have an—explanation— for all of my actions.'

'I've heard it!' she retorted. 'You've got your head so full of your mistress that it really gummed up the works when Joanna came home before the wedding. You needed to be married, and . . .'

'I needed to marry you, I'll agree,' Cale said quietly, 'but there's another—explanation—of which you know nothing.'

'Naturally, it'll be as devious as all your other explanations.' She refused to let up.

'No,' he denied flatly. 'But, since it looks as though the hour of—my having to tell you all that there is to tell has been forced upon me—and since this may take some time— we might both do better if we sat down.'

'You're sure you don't want coffee with it?' Anstey offered sarcastically, and weathered his waiting look.

But she did not want to sit down. Nor did she want to listen to any explanation either. Cale was more than capable of sifting through problems and having the answers in a few seconds flat—she'd seen him do that very thing when she'd told him that grandmothers would forgive everything to be presented with their first grandchild. He'd driven from Hampshire to London since she had taken off, which gave him plenty of time in which to permutate any explanation a hundred different ways.

Her stubborn refusal to be seated, however, was countered by Cale's waiting silence. And suddenly, if reluctantly, Anstey found she was mumbling, 'Are you going to lie to me?'

'I shall tell you nothing but the truth,' Cale promised her firmly.

'And—there won't be anything devious . . . or guaranteed to lead me up the garden path in your explanation?'

'You have my word.'

Anstey, reluctant still, took the nearest seat, which happened to be the settee. When Cale joined her there, she almost stood up again because, accomplished manipulator though she knew him to be, his nearness still had the power to affect her. Afraid, though, that he might see what without so much as touching her he could do to her, she made herself remain where she was. But, in contrast to how she was feeling, her voice was sharp when she challenged,

'So—explain away. Explain why, if it wasn't on account of your mistress—when you *knew* there would be no wedding if Joanna came home first, you *deliberately* had me kept in ignorance that Joanna had turned up. Not only had me deliberately kept in ignorance,' she built up a full head of steam, 'but, when you knew that the—the whole "mess" had been cleared up, you allowed me to go ahead and marry you. And,' she added, 'don't try to tell me that you hadn't seen Joanna and Lester until today, because I heard *both* of them say that you'd told them not to come to St James's. Which has to mean you saw them before today!'

She ran out of steam, but that did not stop her from

glaring at him. She half expected him to fire back something short and sharp in return. But, having experienced Cale at his arrogant worst, she was surprised when he stated calmly, 'I've said I shall tell you only the truth, Anstey, and I shall. To begin with, when I saw Lester on Wednesday ...'

'Wednesday!' Anstey pounced. 'You've known since *Wednesday* that Lester and ... While I was trying to phone you to cancel everything, you were ...'

'You tried to ring me on Wednesday—to cancel our wedding?'

'And on Tuesday too,' she wasted no time to tell him. 'Only you were too busy elsewhere, I presume, to answer your phone.' Oh grief, she swallowed, had she sounded jealous?

She saw a smile start to appear on Cale's mouth, and suddenly she decided that she did not find his smile so endearing after all. That hint of a smile had faded though, when he told her levelly, 'I was busy both on Tuesday and Wednesday, with matters down at Quiet Ways. But,' he added, 'perhaps it's just as well that my mother rang on Tuesday in something of a state.'

If by that he meant that by not being at his apartment to take her call, he had been saved from trying to talk her out of cancelling their wedding, then Anstey did not thank him for it.

'I can understand your mother being in a state,' she told him stonily instead. 'She must have been quite bewildered when Joanna and Lester turned up and claimed as theirs the baby she had believed to be yours and mine.'

'My mother knew the truth before Joanna and Lester appeared,' Cale enlightened her. 'They didn't arrive at Quiet Ways until Wednesday—she knew the truth on Tuesday.'

'You—told her?' she questioned, starting to grow confused.

'She'd more or less guessed,' he replied.

'She'd guessed! But—how? I didn't give a thing away, I'm sure I didn't. And you,' she said a trifle acidly, 'you're too sharp ever to be caught out.'

Cale received her acid comment unblinkingly, and proceeded to tell her, 'Apparently, having attained her heart's wish—that you and I marry—it left her with time to puzzle into what she had observed, but hadn't previously dwelt too deeply upon. When she rang on Tuesday, and began by saying that she was so happy that you and I were to marry, and added that, while she could quite well believe Lester capable of allowing a child of his to be born illegitimate, it was entirely out of keeping with what she knew of me—I smelt trouble.'

'On just that?' Anstey queried.

'There was more,' Cale agreed, 'but just the fact that she had mentioned Lester's name for the first time since their quarrel came to light told me she had the bit well and truly between her teeth.'

'You said there was more?'

'There was. Idly, it seemed, she referred to the fact of Lester having inherited the Yoxhall toes, but how I had not.'

'You haven't got two toes joined together!' Anstey exclaimed, somehow having taken it for granted that he had.

He shook his head. 'When she went probing on to state that while she didn't know very much about genes, it struck her as most odd that Rosie should have inherited the Yoxhall toes, not from her father, but from her uncle, I knew that I had to tell her the truth.'

'You told her over the phone?'

Again Cale shook his head. 'I didn't want to tell her at all,

not then,' he admitted. 'But when she enquired if you knew
Lester, and I saw which way her mind was working, well,'
he paused, 'I couldn't have that. I told her I was on my
way.'

Anstey's heart gave a little flip at Cale's intimation that,
to protect her name, he had gone to confess the truth to his
mother. But she negated any softening that intimation had
brought. There was still a lot of explaining she wanted from
Cale Quartermaine.

'So, you went straight away to see her,' she said flatly, but
discovered that she wanted to know, 'How did she take it?'

'She was half-way adjusted to knowing the truth before I
confirmed it,' Cale replied. 'At that time I didn't know that
Joanna and Lester were together, or where either of them
were, but one half-shock a day in my judgement was
enough for a lady of my mother's years. Since she was soon
asking the question—where were Rosie's parents?—I told
her something of what you had told me of Joanna's
miserable childhood. While she was murmuring sympa-
thetically over that, I told her that Joanna had run away,
and that Lester had run to try and find her. Little did I
know then,' he ended, 'how near to the truth I was.'

'Lester went looking for Joanna!' Anstey exclaimed,
utterly astonished. 'But he didn't even know she'd
disappeared!' she protested, and was suddenly very
distrustful of Cale and his assurances that he would tell her
only the truth. 'I told you myself how I'd tried, without
success, to contact him,' she said bluntly. 'Never once, since
she went, did he call at the flat. He couldn't even be
bothered to pick up a phone to enquire if she was feeling
better when he *must* have known how much he'd upset her
the last time they spoke. So you tell me,' she snapped
hostilely, 'how did he know that she'd gone away?'

Cale studied her hostile expression, and then, quite
simply, he said, 'Through you.'

'Through me! Don't give me that!' she scoffed angrily. 'I've only just finished telling you, I didn't even know where Lester worked, so how could I ...'

'The way I heard it,' he cut in, 'you were so worried that Joanna was in the throes of post-natal depression that you went to see her doctor. A—Dr Favell—is that right?'

Her determination not to believe another word Cale said took a severe blow. Not only did he know she had been to see Joanna's doctor, when she was sure that she hadn't told him, but he also knew Dr Favell's name!

'I didn't go to see him about Joanna!' she gasped. 'I was worried about Rosie because she never seemed to stop crying. Though, come to think of it,' she recalled, 'I did tell him that Joanna was unhappy and that she had gone away. I also told him,' she said slowly, 'what a rat Lester was, and how he was the cause of Joanna's deep unhappiness. But— he never said anything to me about suspecting that Joanna might be suffering from post-natal depression. Grief!' she exclaimed, 'I'd have got the police out to find her if I'd thought she was ...'

'She wasn't,' Cale cut in quietly, and even smiled gently at her concern, before he went on. 'But this Dr Favell was sufficiently disturbed by what you'd told him to not want to take any chances. He decided it wouldn't hurt to give my brother something of a jolt.'

'He contacted him?' Anstey asked, wide-eyed.

'Lester—name, address and phone number—was listed on his records as Joanna's next of kin. In his favour, Lester was feeling the pangs of conscience about what he'd said to Joanna over the phone, and before the doctor rang was fighting a compulsion to go to her. When Dr Favell phoned and embroidered his fears for her safety—telling him she had been hysterical when she'd disappeared—Lester's jealousy of his baby daughter became insignificant.'

'He was jealous of Rosie!'

'Lester is used to being adored,' Cale shrugged. 'He felt his mother had rejected him, and felt more and more pushed out when Joanna, delighted to discover she was pregnant, lost no opportunity to talk about her forthcoming event whenever they met.'

'Good heavens!' murmured Anstey. 'But go on—what happened after . . .'

'After Dr Favell put the frighteners on? That part was easy. Lester's fight not to go to Joanna disappeared without trace. He thought he knew where to find her, and went hot-foot straight to a place where he and Joanna had once spent an idyllic weekend.'

'She was there?'

Cale nodded. 'Lester was devastated at how pale and drawn she looked. He straight away asked her to marry him, and was beside himself when she refused.'

'She refused? But she loves him! She . . .'

'Of course she loves him,' Cale smiled. 'Why else would she agree to his next suggestion that, before they finally parted, they should spend a platonic holiday together—for old times' sake.'

'They went away—on holiday—together!' Each sentence Cale uttered was more surprising than the last.

'Lester looked on it more as a convalescence for Joanna,' Cale told her, and caused Anstey's heart to flip yet again when he added gently, 'While you, my dear, were tearing your hair out trying to find a way to cope, Joanna, her only confidence at that time being that whatever else happened, you wouldn't let her down and that she could trust you with her baby, went on holiday with my brother to the South of France.'

'Th-then—Lester must really love Joanna?'

'He sold his car to pay for the holiday, and hired another. A step he wouldn't normally take.'

'But they're not going to get married?'

'They are.' Seeing that she looked confused, Cale explained, 'By the time their return ferry docked at Portsmouth, they were the best of friends. So much so that, by then anxious to get back to her baby, Joanna told Lester that she would go to London but, as he was so near to his mother's home, she thought it was about time that he went and made his peace.'

'He'd have told Joanna about the quarrel at some time during the holiday, I expect,' Anstey suggested, knowing full well that Joanna had not known before.

'Must have,' he agreed, and went on, 'But by then Lester didn't want Joanna out of his sight. He told her he'd go and see his mother, but only if she went with him.'

'Joanna consented, and—on Wednesday—they arrived at Quiet Ways,' Anstey filled in, her fascination with all Cale had been telling her starting to dip as anger with him started to surge up again. 'Where,' she added, 'your mother already knew that they were Rosie's parents.'

'That's right.' Cale's eyes were steady on hers, so he couldn't miss the knowledge that he was sailing towards choppy waters. 'When all greetings, apologies and so forth were over, Lester, tickled pink to hold his child in his arms, promptly asked Joanna how she could think of allowing her daughter to grow up without a father. Joanna, in tears, I believe, accepted his second proposal.'

For a moment Anstey felt a little moist-eyed herself on Joanna's behalf. But not for very long. She remembered once thinking that she had wanted neither Mrs Quartermaine nor Joanna to be hurt by any of this, but never then had she suspected that she would be the one to end up hurting the most. And, hurt, she went for Cale.

'So all the Quartermaines end up happily!' she snapped shortly. 'Naturally, nobody thought to give me a ring to tell *me* what was happening!'

'Of course they did!' Cale said sharply. 'I very nearly had

to disconnect the phone to stop Joanna putting through a call to you.'

'I should have guessed!' Anstey said with hot sarcasm, realising that none of what he had so far told her explained any of his treachery. 'What sort of devious line did you have to feed her, to stop her phoning? You were busy with matters down at Quiet Ways both on Tuesday *and* Wednesday, I think you said.'

Cale didn't look too impressed with her memory, although he did confess, 'While they were up in the nursery, my mother rang to tell me that Lester had found Joanna, and that they were both there.'

'She—tipped you off!' Anstey gasped incredulously, and not giving him a chance to reply, while at the same time she wondered where her brain had been all this time, 'My sainted aunt!' she exclaimed. 'You told your mother the truth about Rosie on Tuesday! She must have known then that there was no reason for us to marry.' Getting more angry by the second, she rushed on, 'Are you trying to tell me that *never once*, since she knew the truth, has your mother asked if she should cancel the wedding cake?'

With the heat of anger flaming in her eyes, Anstey refused to look away from Cale's steady gaze. When he seemed to hesitate over his reply, she would dearly have liked to have known what was going on in his head. But she was as wary as ever to any sidetracking answer he might have dreamed up, when he at last replied.

'She wouldn't be the woman I know her to be, if she hadn't put one or two pertinent questions,' he said slowly.

'Pertinent questions which, of course, while conveying that you wanted the wedding to go ahead, you were able to answer without revealing that the only reason you wanted to be married was because of your married mistress.'

Again Cale hesitated, and seemed almost to square his shoulders, before quietly, he let fall, 'In point of fact,

Anstey—there is no married mistress.'

Shaken to hear something she had not expected to hear, Anstey looked at him blankly. She was still blinking and of the view that he'd given her enough of a run-around, when she questioned, 'She's not married? But you definitely told me that . . .'

'Forget what I told you,' Cale interrupted her flow. 'I admit I lied to you, but if you'll let me, I shall tell you only the truth from now on.'

'Far be it from me to prevent this new you from appearing,' Anstey told him stiffly, and, continuing in the same acid vein, 'So, your mistress either did a quick execution job on her husband, got herself smartly divorced, or was never married to begin w . . .'

'I have no mistress—widowed, divorced, or single,' Cale cut her off curtly. His voice had softened, though, when he revealed, Since I met you, Anstey, I've had no time for other women.'

Anstey saw a look of warmth in his eyes, and for a few seconds she allowed herself to idiotically believe what, astoundingly, Cale was saying. Her heartbeat returned to normal when she realised that, since his weekends were spent in shuttling her to Quiet Ways and back, as he had just said, it left him no time for other women.

The coldness that smote her heart was in her voice too when, certain that her question was going to throw him, she challenged, 'Why then, with the truth about Rosie out, with Lester and your mother reconciled, why, if there isn't a cuckold husband somewhere, did you go through that wedding ceremony with me today?'

Cale was not thrown, but Anstey was. For the eyes that looked steadily into hers never wavered, when he replied, 'I married you today, Anstey, because I had to. I married you—because it was my dearest wish to make you—my wife.'

Her throat went dry. Incapable of speech, she searched his eyes, which seemed to be seeking some kind of encouragement from hers. She had no idea how long she teetered on the brink of believing that his astonishing statement meant just what it said. But even as her heart drummed so loudly that she thought he might hear it, some stunned part of her brain was stirring and began to urge 'He's up to something—don't trust him'.

Tearing her gaze from him, she found it easier to think when she was not looking at him. It was then that she realised it would be the height of folly to take his 'I married you—because it was my dearest wish to make you—my wife' at face value. Past experience showed that Cale was a master in the art of leading a false trail.

Her heartbeat had evened out when, determined not to be taken in again, she muttered, 'This is going to be good,' and, flicking him an icy glance, 'You do, I take it,' she enquired with acid sweetness, 'have a well-laid explanation for your last remark?'

He did not like her tone, or her attitude, she could tell that from the way he frowned darkly at her. 'There's nothing well-laid, or previously thought out, in what I have to tell you,' he fired shortly.

'You must be slipping!' Anstey snapped back. 'You think quicker than ...'

'It wasn't a case of slipping,' he chopped her off brusquely, and though she had only ever known him as a man sure of himself, he seemed strangely unsure when he added, 'It was more a case of—falling.'

Anstey knew that she had to keep her wits about her where he was concerned, but already she felt befuddled. 'I'd appreciate fewer of the conundrums, and more of the facts,' she told him bluntly.

'You're not—making this easy for me, Anstey,' he told her grittily.

'Good,' she said hard-heartedly. But her hard-heartedness was phoney, and her softer feelings for him made it impossible for her to keep it up. She remembered how he had once told her to start at the beginning, and unbent sufficiently to invite carelessly, 'How about taking it from the beginning?'

'Why not?' he agreed to her surprise. Then he further surprised her by revealing that the beginning commenced from the day she had gone to his office. 'To start,' he told her, 'no bundle of blonde-headed dynamite had ever stormed my office before, and taken a swing at me. It is not something,' he added, his eyes as steady as ever on her face, 'which a man easily forgets.'

'I—er—like to leave my mark,' murmured Anstey, confused to know what the point was he was leading up to.

'You did that and no mistake,' Cale told her solemnly. 'I own, Anstey, that I'd never come across a woman quite like you before.'

'I try to be different,' she threw in off-handedly.

'You don't "try" anything,' he contradicted her sharply. 'You're just—you—naturally.' Not sure if she had just been served a compliment, Anstey decided to stay quiet, and, his sharp tone gone, Cale continued, 'You stayed in my mind long after you'd left my office that day.'

'On account of the way I hit you?' Despite her having decided not to say another word until he had delivered his planned explanation, Anstey found her tongue betraying her.

'That's what I told myself,' he replied, but smiled as he revealed, 'There was no end to the self-deception I put up in those early days of knowing you.'

'Really?' she queried, striving like mad to make her voice sound only vaguely interested, but her thoughts flying to find what construction she should put on what he had just said.

'Really,' he replied. 'You were still in my head the following day, so naturally,' he said with a self-derisory shrug, 'I realised that while it was one thing to decide I'd done with getting Lester out of scrapes—you, and his offspring, were another.'

'You came to this flat, that Tuesday, because you discovered that you couldn't stand by and do nothing about Rosie,' Anstey got herself together to document.

'I did,' Cale agreed. 'But only to be aware as I left you that there were forces at work within me that were far outside my experience.'

'You—er—didn't know w-what those forces were?'

'I wouldn't admit them for what they were even when recognition came hammering on my door,' he told her quietly. 'It seemed no more than natural to admire your courage in doing all you could to keep my niece safe for your friend, so I shied away from—and even fought against—the emotion I felt for you but didn't want to name.'

'Y-you—said that—you liked me,' she reminded him.

'And I do,' he replied softly. 'You have a tender heart, and I like that. I like the way you smile and the way you laugh. Even, believe it or not, I like the way you look as haughty as hell just before you tear into me about something.'

'I look haughty sometimes?' Anstey exclaimed.

'Didn't you know?'

She shook her head, 'I've often thought of you as an arrogant devil, but I didn't know . . .'

'A lesser man would run for cover at the first sign of your haughty look,' Cale smiled. And, perhaps emboldened by the fact that Anstey had to smile in return, he quite out of the blue all but caused her to collapse, when he said quietly, 'Is it any wonder that I not only like you but—love you, my dear?'

Shaken, wide-eyed, not fully crediting what she thought she had just heard, Anstey began to tremble. 'D-did you say—that . . .' she had to swallow hard before she could continue, ' . . . that you love me?'

'I did, and I do.' His eyes were intent on her when he told her, 'At first, all I knew was that I felt good inside when I was with you. Then I began to feel good inside *only* when I was with you. I've fought this emotion you've unearthed in me,' he owned and, reaching to take a hold of one of her hands, seemed encouraged when her trembling communicated itself to him. 'I told myself that I enjoyed being a bachelor,' he continued. 'But when thoughts of you began to dominate my every waking moment, I realised that I was going to have to do something about it. By fair means, or by foul, my dear, dear Anstey, I had to make you my wife.'

'You m-married me—because you—love me?' she asked huskily. 'It wasn't because your mistress . . .'

'There is no mistress,' he stated firmly. 'I . . .'

Suddenly though, Anstey did not want to hear any more. If he could lie about that, he could lie about anything! Hurriedly, she snatched her hand out of his grasp. 'And if I believe that, I'll believe in Santa Claus,' she snapped. 'You've used me for your own purposes from the beginning. I refuse,' she said agitatedly, 'to be used ever again. I don't care what your motive in this . . .'

'My only motive . . .'

'Your only motive is one which no doubt I shall hear about in the fullness of time,' Anstey cut him off speedily. Suddenly though, it dawned on her that he must know she had some feeling for him, or why else would he use his supposed 'love' as a lever? Alarmed, she quickly found a panicky sort of sarcasm to rush on to jibe, 'While I appreciate that it's probably your style not to tell your bride you love her until *after* the wedding ceremony, this bride doesn't give a button anyway.'

'You don't . . .!' Cale broke off, and looked truly shaken. But even while Anstey was discounting his shaken look, and was adding 'actor' to his list of accomplishments, he was rubbing a hand across his nape, and was muttering, 'Hell—I didn't dare risk it. As it is, I've been holding my breath in fear that my mother's sense of right and wrong would yet see her ring you.'

'You thought she would telephone—to tell me that she knew everything?' Anstey was surprised enough to ask.

'Her gratitude for all you did for her granddaughter was such that, on Tuesday, she wanted to immediately get on the phone to you.'

'Good heavens!' Anstey gasped. 'So that's what she meant when she said "Thank you" this morning!' She saw Cale's slightly perplexed look, but instead of explaining, she recovered to ask, 'But you stopped her from phoning me?'

'I did,' he admitted. 'I told her that if she had any feeling for me at all, any wish in her heart to see her elder son get anywhere near to his heart's desire, then she wouldn't say a word to you about knowing the truth.'

'You . . .' she began, and suddenly found she did not want to heed the warning of her head that he must have some other devious motive. 'You . . .' she started off again, but had to clear a small constriction in her throat, before she could ask, 'Would you mind telling me what else you told your mother?'

'I told her that I was desperately in love with you,' he willingly obliged. 'I told her that above all else, I wanted to marry you, and would marry you, but that she could ruin everything for me if she breathed a word about knowing that Lester and Joanna were Rosie's parents.'

She started to tremble anew, and question after question popped into her head. But she had to swallow again too, before she could ask, 'Y-your mother—she agreed to k-keep silent—just like that?'

'You know her better than that,' Cale answered with a hint of a smile, but his look was sincere when he said, 'But she agreed not to interfere after I'd answered all her questions, and even rang me as soon as she could after Joanna and Lester turned up.'

'You—went down straight away after her call?'

'My foot was flat to the boards until I reached Quiet Ways,' he replied, and did not wait for her to ask what happened then, but told her, 'By the time I got there, Joanna and Lester were engaged to be married and my mother, as you might imagine, had Mr Midwinter scheduled to dine that evening. But first I had to listen to an account of Joanna and Lester's doings. Then, having observed that my brother appeared to have grown up and seemed eager to shoulder his responsibilities, I told them that you and I had met through Rosie. Joanna, incidentally, was thrilled when I told her that you and I were to be married today, and . . .'

'You said you almost had to disconnect the phone to stop her from ringing me.'

'So I did,' Cale remembered grimly. 'I'd hoped, by telling her of the traumatic time you'd had of it in keeping her child safe for her, that she'd see how, in this time of you getting ready for your wedding in a hurry, you wouldn't have time to speak to her on the phone. When that didn't work and she said she'd ring you at the office on Elton Diesel time, I had to tell her that you'd given your job up, and that you were staying with friends of mine.'

Wide-eyed, her heart going like an express train, 'You lied to her?' Anstey asked.

'For you, Anstey Quartermaine, to be married to you today, I was ready to lie to anyone,' Cale said gently though he added quickly, 'But I'm not lying to you now Nor shall I, ever again.'

Anstey was ready to wilt, but she knew that there was something else she wanted to ask him. When Cale took hold of her hand as if in need of some small physical contact with her, she had the hardest job in the world to remember what her question was. She looked away from him, and more by luck than anything else, the question was there.

'You tried to get Joanna and Lester not to show up today—er—how . . .'

'I thought I'd succeeded.' Cale read her question. 'I realised that Lester must be without an income when he said he'd sold his car to raise some funds. Using the trauma they'd put you through for not wanting them at our wedding today, I privately told him that if he'd keep Joanna away, I'd reinstate him—not in his old job—but at his old salary.'

'He agreed?' Anstey queried, accepting that, when pushed, there was no end to what Cale would do.

'Like a shot,' he confirmed. 'They booked into a hotel, leaving the baby at Quiet Ways, and I thought I was over another hurdle.'

'Only—you weren't.'

'I'd reckoned without the power of Lester's love for Joanna,' Cale admitted. 'After you'd sped off in the Rolls I looked for some transport to come after you. Lester must have read my mind, because he had his car running and the passenger door open ready to speed to collect my car. My car is faster than the model he has on hire,' he paused to insert, and continued, 'I was only half hearing what he said as we raced for The Carpenter's, but the gist of it was that after he'd treated Joanna the way he had, he could not deny her her wish to see you married. Also, could he still have the job I'd promised?'

'What did you tell him?'

'I told him,' said Cale, and seemed suddenly on edge, 'that if I'd lost you, there was no question—he had definitely lost his job.'

'Oh—Cale!' Anstey sighed tremulously.

'Does—does that mean—I have a chance?' he asked, his voice suddenly thick in his throat. And when Anstey was too stunned by the raw emotion in him to find her voice, 'Tell me, for God's sake,' he urged hoarsely, 'have I blown everything by the way I've been—or is there a chance that the love I once thought I saw in your eyes is what I thought it, and not just what I wanted to see?'

'Y-you—didn't—imagine it.'

'You do feel something for me, other than—hate?'

'Would I have married a man I hated?'

'Would you?' he demanded.

'I—love you,' Anstey told him, and suddenly she was in his arms.

'Oh, God,' Cale breathed, 'how you've made me suffer!' He pulled back, his eyes adoring on her face. 'Never put me through a time like that again,' he muttered, and pulled her up against him again.

'I won't.' Anstey promised, and had her lips claimed in a gentle kiss.

'I haven't been as nervous as that since I took my first school exam,' murmured Cale, and only then did she realise the strain he had been under in case she did not love him.

Then he kissed her again, and she was not aware of any coherent thought as again they kissed, and clung, as though starved of each other. But, gradually, Cale's kisses gentled out.

'Oh, my sweet love,' he said softly, 'you can have no idea of the mental torment you've put me through.'

'Torment?' she queried chokily.

'Torment, my love,' he repeated, his look tender on her emotion-filled eyes. 'I didn't comprehend what was happening to me to begin with. It happened so fast,' he explained, 'this ache to be with you, this ache to see you smile, to hear your laugh.' Anstey sighed happily, and Cale, after planting a light kiss on the end of her nose, went on, 'The first indication I received that I'd better sharpen up was at dinner that first evening at Quiet Ways, when my mother went surging ahead with her plans to get us married. The very idea of my bachelor self being married should, I later realised, have horrified me. But I could recall no feeling of horror.'

'You—did later?'

'Warning trumpets had been sounded,' he grinned. 'I should have known, when we drove back to London, without the infant, that it was already too late. That didn't prevent me from trying to eject you from my mind, though.'

'Was that why you were like a bear with a sore head when I rang to ask for your mother's telephone number?'

'By that Tuesday I was not only trying to get you out of my mind, but was having to contend with feelings of jealousy too.'

'You were jealous!' Anstey exclaimed. 'But—of whom? I didn't have any particular manfriend just then!'

'That's what made me so irritable with not only you, but myself. There didn't have to be any one man! Just the fact that you were a beautiful woman and must have scores of men friends was enough for me to have to call on you that evening to see for myself whom you were entertaining.'

'Oh, Cale!' Anstey whispered.

He kissed her lightly, and confessed, 'It felt so good, just to be with you that night, that I just had to kiss you before I left. One kiss wasn't enough.'

A little shyly, she took up, 'And I went to pieces when I saw the frame with Joanna and Lester's picture in, and I knew that it just wasn't right for us to—make love, when we weren't in love like they had been.'

'My sweet lovely,' murmured Cale. 'I left your flat in a rage, and spent the rest of the time until I called for you on

Friday in drumming up a loathing for the sort of tease you were. Useless, of course,' he smiled. 'It was so good to be with you again that by the time I went to bed on Friday night, I had to face the fact that I was so much in love with you that I just had to marry you.'

'You knew you loved me then!'

He nodded. 'Only you were being so aloof, I didn't think I stood a chance. Then you were all upset that your rights regarding Joanna's baby were slipping from you, and suddenly there did seem a chance. I grabbed it. I found the nerve to suggest that to marry me would be an answer.'

'That was on Saturday after lunch,' Anstey remembered clearly. Just as she remembered, 'It was that afternoon I realised just why I couldn't get you out of my head either, and just why it was you had the power to throw my emotions out of gear. I took myself off for a walk, and realised that I was in love with you.'

'My darling!' Cale breathed, and nothing was said after that for some minutes as he cradled her in his arms, and Anstey clung to him. They kissed and broke apart, and after some moments spent in getting herself more of one piece, she told him,

'It must have been my love for you which tripped me up when I told your mother that not only had you proposed but that I had accepted you. I was horrified the moment the words slipped out,' she owned.

'And I,' Cale said tenderly, 'couldn't have been more delighted. Especially when to jump to my defence the way you did seemed to indicate that you must like me a little. I was ready to snatch at any straw in that direction,' he confessed, and went on to tell her, 'Whether my mother and Lester ever became reconciled was by then a side issue. I wanted your love so badly that when the next day you came into the dining-room and I imagined I saw love in your eyes, I very nearly risked everything there and then.

and took you in my arms.'

'You remembered in time that your mother and the vicar were there in the same room?'

He shook his head. 'You suddenly went cold on me, and instinct to believe you felt something for me began to wage war with a stronger instinct which warned not to make any move which could frighten you off. I became plain scared,' he freely owned, 'that I could easily ruin what small chance I had with you.'

'Oh, Cale!' sighed Anstey.

His right hand caressed the side of her face, and with his loved-filled look on her eyes, he went on to explain, 'For years, my love, I've pushed ahead in business and taken what chances I've had to to achieve my goals. It's second nature to me to go after what I want and to take on board any risk involved. When to marry you became the greatest goal of my life, and I saw a chance to do just that—I took it. But, Anstey, my heart, to tell you how it was with me was one risk I didn't dare take.'

'Oh, darling!' she cried, her heart full at the depth of love he must have for her. Cale had nerves of steel in business, yet he had been so afraid in love. Suddenly she just had to tell him, 'You'd have had no doubts about my feelings for you if you'd known the agony of jealousy I've been through over your non-existent married lady-friend.'

'Forgive me, sweetheart,' Cale said swiftly, but smiled ruefully as he owned, 'I was so overjoyed inside that our marriage was arranged that, on our drive back to London last Sunday, I forgot entirely that ours was not a normal engagement. So overjoyed, and forgetful, in fact, that it wasn't until you asked why I wanted to marry you that I was made to remember, and made to wonder—had I given away that I was in love with you?'

'You hadn't,' Anstey told him dreamily.

'I know that now,' he said softly, 'but at the time I soon

realised from your tone that if you had seen my love you didn't want it. I knew then that, if I told you the truth about why I wanted to marry you, there was every chance you'd at once call the wedding off. I couldn't have that,' he murmured, 'so I had to think fast.'

'You—wretch,' she smiled.

Cale laughed as he told her, 'I thought I heard jealousy in your voice when I rang you last night. It gave me tremendous heart. I'd wanted some communication with you all week,' he said tenderly, 'but after you slammed the phone down on me on Monday, I knew that one wrong move and my one chance to marry you would be gone. I've been treading on eggs ever since everything blew up at Quiet Ways on Tuesday and Wednesday,' he confessed, and added, 'I was never so relieved when you asked if Ted was driving me to the church. I took it as confirmation that you would be there too, and still intended to marry me. Fear that in my jubilation I might give myself away made me hang up quickly.'

Again they kissed, and Anstey was breathless when Cale pulled back and saw her starry-eyed look.

'Oh, Anstey, my heart,' he breathed, 'I love you so.'

'I love you, Cale,' Anstey told him threadily, but her voice was stronger when, albeit a shade hesitantly, she asked, 'Would you have—told me all you have—if I hadn't run away?'

'I can't truthfully say,' he owned honestly, 'but I hoped that a month alone together, away from family and friends, might . . .'

'A month!' she exclaimed. 'But I only agreed to a weekend, to . . .'

'What sort of husband do you think I am, that I'd limit our honeymoon to a weekend?' Cale enquired, clearly enjoying her amazement. 'I've a plane standing by to take us to an island from where there are no return flights unless especially ordered.' Anstey was still savouring the word 'honeymoon', when he added, 'You once caused my plans a serious setback by categorically refusing to move in and live with me when we were married. Tell me, wife,' he said with mock severity, 'do you still stand by that statement?'

Anstey burst out laughing; she couldn't help it. She was in love with Cale, he was in love with her. The look in his eyes as he drew her to her feet told her that he liked the sound of her laughter. But her laughter had gone, when sincerely she replied to his question.

'I should like, very, very much,' she told him softly, 'to move in and live with you.'

'Good,' he said, his tone telling her he would have accepted no other reply. 'And you no longer wish to divorce me?' he asked, everything about him stating that she hadn't got a prayer in that direction anyway.

'I no longer wish to divorce you,' Anstey answered solemnly.

Gently Cale kissed her, and as he set her from him, he had one other thing to say to her before he took her to their honeymoon island.

'Then will you please me, Mrs Quartermaine,' he requested, 'by returning your wedding ring to the finger on which, with all the love in my heart, I placed it.'

'Oh, Cale!' Anstey cried and, now aware that he had felt the same love as she when they had exchanged their vows, she willingly obeyed his request.

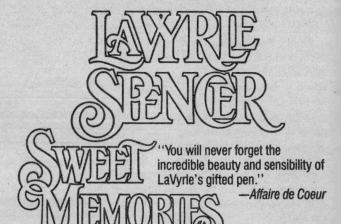

ATTRACTIVE, SPACE SAVING BOOK RACK

Display your most prized novels on this handsome and sturdy book rack. The hand-rubbed walnut finish will blend into your library decor with quiet elegance, providing a practical organizer for your favorite hard-or soft-covered books.

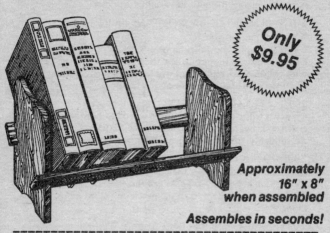

Only $9.95

Approximately 16" x 8" when assembled

Assembles in seconds!

To order, rush your name, address and zip code, along with a check or money order for $10.70* ($9.95 plus 75¢ postage and handling) payable to *Harlequin Reader Service*:

Harlequin Reader Service
Book Rack Offer
901 Fuhrmann Blvd.
P.O. Box 1396
Buffalo, NY 14269-1396

Offer not available in Canada.

BKR-1A

*New York and Iowa residents add appropriate sales tax.

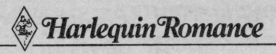
Harlequin Romance

Coming Next Month

Available in July wherever paperback books are sold, or through Harlequin Reader Service:

In the U.S.
901 Fuhrmann Blvd.
P.O. Box 1397
Buffalo, N.Y. 14240-1397

In Canada
P.O. Box 603
Fort Erie, Ontario
L2A 5X3

COMING THIS JULY

Harlequin Historicals

*Storytelling at its best
by some of your favorite authors such as
Kristen James, Nora Roberts, Cassie Edwards*

Strong, independent heroines
Heroes you'll fall in love with
Compelling love stories

History has never been so romantic.

Look for them in July wherever Harlequin Books are sold.